3 NBs of Julian Drew

3 NBs of Julian Drew

James M. Deem

Houghton Mifflin Company
Boston 1994

Library of Congress Cataloging-in-Publication Data

Deem, James M.
3 NBs of Julian Drew / by James M. Deem.
p. cm.
Summary: The journals of a troubled fifteen-year-old boy who lives with his father and emotionally and physically abusive stepmother and her children after the death of his own mother years ago.
ISBN 0-395-69453-1
[1. Family problems — Fiction. 2. Stepfamilies — Fiction. 3. Mothers — Fiction. 4. Death — Fiction. 5. Friendship — Fiction. 6. Diaries — Fiction.] I. Title. II. Title: Three NBs of Julian Drew. III. Title: Three notebooks of Julian Drew.
PZ7.D3594Aaf 1994 93-39306
[Fic] — dc20 CIP
AC

Printed in the United States of America

BP 10 9 8 7 6 5 4 3 2 1

From my H
w/L
4 S +
of course my M
— JD

3 NBs of Julian Drew

NB #1:

The
1M155U
NB

TO25
427WP
can't

can

have 2

my eyes saw

Ur letter

in my dream

in MY dream

IN MY DREAM

+

my MM bought

this

NB

2day

2DAY

JD

WO26
414WP

The lock is on

my hand is trying 2 write

trying

        TRYING 2 write

my brain dreamed about Ur letter

4

20

nights

until last night

now no dream

no dream now

no

   dream

          now

the lock

is

on

JD

SO29
217WA

Dear

Deer who?
Why won't my pen do this?
know why?
no why?
Everything is like watching myself in a mirror
My eyes are tired of mirror-watching me
My eyes are tired
but my hand is trying.

Julian

MO31
742WP

My brain is thinking of some 1.
It is thinking of U.
Me + U
My brain can't stand it
Anymore
4 yr is a long time. 4 yr is 4ever.

All it thinks about is U.
Or THEM.
Don't think about THEM, brain.
Just think about U.

Julian

THN3
415WP

My hand is going 2 WRITE.
My hand IS going 2 write.
My hand is going 2 write U if it K1775 me.
No 1 can stop me.
43 can't stop me.
543 can't stop me.
There are 2 many things 2 write.
2 many.

My hand will write 1 THING.
Some THING my brain thinks about.

My brain had a nowhere dream 4 20 nights. My body was nowhere.
It was dusty, smelly, old.

My eyes saw a book on a shelf. It was Ur book.
My fingers found a letter inside.

The letter was from U.
It was so real my ears heard the envelope crackle.
My nose could smell Ur perfume.

But the dream stopped be4 my eyes could read the letter + now my brain doesn't dream this dream anymore.

What was inside the letter? What did U want 2 tell me?

My hand wrote
2 many
things
(maybe it's the pen's fault).

Julian

SN5
349WP

This NB is green
80-page spiral w/34 lines on a page
5440 lines total 2 write on.

This NB says Econo-line on the cover.

This NB was purchased 335WP TO25 in Osco Drug at Mercado Plaza on University Dr.

My brain wants 2 remember everything about it.

The cashier w/the Janice nametag waited on me. She was wearing a T-shirt that said (2 me) 170V3 Rick. My brain was wondering what it would be like 2 be Rick. My brain was playing crazy thoughts.
Only Janice 7OV35 Rick, not me.
A me w/o U.

Julian

MN7
407WP

Dear XXXXX,

My hand wrote Ur name (even if the pen crossed it out). Then the pen drew a box around each letter + wrote every letter of the alphabet on top of each letter in Ur name just 2 make sure no 1 can tell what was there.

Just in case.

Writing Ur name was like seeing Ur face + holding Ur hand. Like talking 2 U again, breathing Ur air. It makes me feel scared. My hand was shaking. My brain was thinking about doing this 4 a long time. My hand decided 2 be a little braver + try this. My hand is going 2 TRY.

2 be braver.

My brain thought about starting (really starting) this NB every day. Could U tell? Writing this is like trying 2 walk after being in a coma since birth. Maybe not birth. Maybe just 4 4 yr. Writing this is like trying 2 talk after having my mouth taped shut 4 4 yr. My hand can't write things that easy. It feels funny. My hand doesn't know what 2 write.

No.

My hand knows what 2 write but the pen won't let it.

Do U understand?

Do U?

What my hand wants 2 write
is hard 2 write
What the pen won't write U is

Maybe my brain could think thoughts 2 U w/o talking + U would know them. But it doesn't know how. All it knows how 2 do is think in secret code. My hand writes secret code 4 some words. Maybe the pen will let me write a secret code just 4 U.

What could my code be?

OK what about this?

The code is: 1M155U.

1 M155 U. Do U understand it?

Here's another: 170V3U.

Now my brain says 2 hide this from THEM.

Maybe there will be more 2morrow if my hand has something 2 say.

Julian

TN8
432WP

Dear U,

This is 4 U, even if the pen won't let me write Ur name. Do U understand? My brain has been thinking about things 2 write U all day. It has 23 things 2 tell U. It remembers them all.

Thing 1: We left WV on A14: 3 yr 6 mo + 25 d ago (do U want 2 know the min + sec?)

Thing 2: 43 drove the car away at 202WA. 543 was right beside 43.

Thing 3: My eyes saw (but no 1s eyes saw me) as we passed under the streetlight at the corner.

Thing 4: My brain could never 4get that time. My brain could never 4get that time was 4bidden.

Thing 5: 43 didn't want the neighbors' eyes 2 see. But U can't ignore the streetlights.

Thing 6: Emma (the only impt person) was sitting in her car seat next 2 me.

Thing 7: Her eyes were C.

Thing 8: We moved 2 Tucson AZ.

Thing 9: It took 17½ d 2 get there.

Thing 10: We had 1 blowout going 70 across MO.

Thing 11: The car broke down near Santa Rosa NM.

Thing 12: We got 2 eat a real dinner there in a real restaurant called the Club Cafe.

Thing 13: We stopped at places 2 sightsee. Indian mounds, petrified forests, meteor craters. All kinds of natural + unnatural disasters.

Thing 14: We have lived in 5 houses in 3 yr + 6 mo + 25 d. Pink, yellow, blue, gray w/red rock in the front yard, + gray w/blue rock.

Thing 15: My body went 2 4 different jr hi schools be4 hi school + now 2 different hi schools. Only they weren't hi schools, they were bye schools. My brain stayed home. As soon as my feet knew the way 2 school, it was time 2 move. 1 day we were there + next we were somewhere else. It was like leaving WV only now we don't leave in the middle of the night.

Thing 16: There are no such things as friends. Just watching + thinking about being friends w/them. Some people seem like they would be nice friends, but their eyes don't see me.

Sometimes it bothers me.

Sometimes it doesn't.

Thing 17: Now we are in Tempe which is next 2 PHX.

Thing 18: We moved here 08.

Thing 19: That means we have been here 26 d + 3 hr + 47 min. That means nothing has changed.

Thing 20: 43 is trying to get lucky in PHX. 43 thinks it will be better here. 43 said no 1 can make a living in Tucson. 43 says the territory is better here. 43 has a new job + only has 2 travel every other wk.

Thing 21: The house we're in now is small, 2 BR + a garage.

Thing 22: Besides Emma + 43 + me, there are 4 people living here now: Roger Rebecca Roxie + 543.

That's all the pen will let me write 4 now.

Except Thing 23: 1M155U.

Julian

WN9
415WP

We are poor. Not like WV where we OWNED a nice house. We're not on food stamps, but there's not much money

4 SOME of US

THEY sold the house + got rid of everything when we moved 2 AZ. We rented a house w/furniture (the pink 1) in Tucson 4 a while but it cost 2 much. So we moved 2 an empty house but there wasn't enough money 4 furniture. Except the couch + coffee table (BUT DONT PUT YOUR FEET ON THEM), the kitchen table + chairs.

Except 1 KINGSIZE BED (+ dresser + chest of drawers).

43 made Emma + the 3Rs (that's Roger Rebecca + Roxie) + me beds out of 2 × 4s + a sheet of plywood

using a plan from some doityourself magazine. Only 43s not very handy + they sagged in the middle. So 43 stacked 4 cinder blocks 2 make a tower under the middle of the plywood 2 hold it up. We didn't even have mattresses 4 them, so we slept in sleeping bags on top of the plywood. A few months ago THEY got Emma Rebecca + Roxie real beds. That's because they're girls. The BOYS still have plywood beds. At night, my ears hear the plywood scraping against the cinder blocks when 1 of us turns over.

My clothes are Kmart shirts (lucky) or outlet shirts (unlucky). They are covered w/sticky XXXs 2 mark the bad spots (but ALL SALES ARE FINAL). My pants are always jeans that are 2 short or 2 loose. My shoes are always 75%-off sneakers.

DONT SAY YOU NEVER GOT ANYTHING.
DONT SAY YOU NEVER GOT

ANY

THING

We keep our clothes in cardboard boxes. Mine are a Lemon Brillo box + a Lemon Joy box. All my clothes smell like lemon soap.

14AT3 lemons but 170V3U

Julian

TN10
416WP

It's hard 4 my hand 2 write 2 U. 2 many things the pen can't tell U. 2 MANY. What if SOMEBODY sees this? What if SOMEBODY finds out? So this NB goes in my DD on the B in the B under everything.

There are things my mouth doesn't talk about w/any 1. There are things my brain doesn't think. There are things, so many THINGS.

Some days it makes me crazy. How can these THINGS stay in my brain? It's like an atomic bomb waiting 2 explode. It is like waiting 2 D.

My hand wants 2 write more 4 U. But it is scared. It told U so much the other day.

Maybe it can write 1 more THING.

1 small thing.

170V3GB

My GB is my garage bedroom (SHARED w/Roger). It's not really a GB, just an old carport that some 1 bricked up (front + back). But it reminds me of our garage in WV.

17OV3GB

It has a concrete floor w/oil stains + cinder block walls. The ceiling is 24 cinder blocks high. There are 816 cinder blocks in the whole room.

There are 4 wooden beams holding up the ceiling.

The ceiling is plywood, painted white.

There are 5 small brown spiders living in the 2 front corners. 3 on the R, 2 on the L.

Sometimes baby lizards crawl through a crack between the cinder blocks in the R rear corner.

The door out of the GB 2 the house has 3 glass window panes. The windows have a curtain inside the house, not on the side of the garage. It used 2 be an outside door.

No. It is still an outside door.

Against the back wall is the old carport storage room. My brain calls it SR, but it's really my (SHARED) closet. SR has a window. If the door 2 SR is open just right, my eyes can look at the back of the house across the alley. Some 1 from my new school lives in that house. That some 1 is S.

17OV3GB + SR

But sometimes my brain thinks about UFOs. It tells my eyes 2 look 4 stars 2 find 1 that moves. Sometimes my brain wants a UFO 2 land in the back yard + take me away.

A big glowing ball would land softly + a door would open. A silver alien would wave 2 me + say: COME HERE, LEAVE THIS PLACE BEHIND. My brain wouldn't think twice about packing. Lemon Brillo boxes are easy 2 carry on2 a spaceship. My brain wouldn't even think once about getting hurt. My ears would hear whatever the alien said. My body would go 2 another planet. My mouth would learn A-talk + eat A-food. My body would sleep in an A-garage + wear cheap A-clothes bought from cheap A-stores 4 the rest of my life. As long as there were new As 2 take care of me.

Sometimes another planet could only be a better place.

My GB doesn't have much furniture. 2 plywood beds + 2 cinder block towers, 2 sleeping bags + pillows, 4 cardboard boxes, + my new desk + chair. Not new really, but new 2 me. Every time we move 2 a house they throw my desk + chair out. This is D4 + C5. It's easier 2 find Cs than Ds. But it's easier 2 make a D out of crates, like the 1 in the pink house.

This time they were sitting in front of a house down the street 1 morning. They were waiting 4 the garbage man. That means me.

543 SAID: THEY MIGHT HAVE BUGS. YOU DONT KNOW WHERE THEYVE BEEN.

170V3 D4 + C5

543 SAID: YOU ALWAYS GO THROUGH OTHER PEOPLES GARBAGE.

14AT3 543

The wood on top of my D is chipped on the edges + some 1 scribbled on the top w/crayons. The drawers are warped + the knobs are loose. The C is made out of molded plastic. The seat is cracked. It has 1 short leg + it wobbles. It doesn't matter what they look like, because they are mine.

The worst part about my GB is it doesn't have any heat; it was in the 40s last night. The other worst part is Roger.

The best part is when no 1 bothers me (which is now when my hand is writing).

My hand has told U a lot (the pen helped).

Do U understand what it means?

1M155U.

Julian

MN14
211WP

My hand couldn't write 4 a few days, because it didn't know what 2 write.

So now it will tell U about school.

14AT3 5C4007

Sophomore

University Hi School

5th wk

bad grades

14AT3 MAT4. My teacher wears old clothes that smell like bad BO. 2day he gave me an F on my homework.

14AT3 59AN154. My teacher gave me an F on my test. Que tal? My body sat there in back of some 1 w/long red hair feeling like my eyes were going 2 C. Instead my brain thought about U.

1M155U. 170V3U.

My brain thinks about U a lot, it thinks about U whenever it feels bad. Which is most of the time now. Sometimes at school (sitting in class) my brain says 2 itself:

1M155U-1M155U-1M155U-1M155U-1M155U
1M155U-1M155U-1M155U-1M155U-1M155U
1M155U-1M155U-1M155U-1M155U-1M155U

My brain says it: One-M-one-five-five-U. It says it over + over like it has magic power. Just like Franny does it in Franny + Zooey, my 2nd favorite book after Catcher in the Rye. She keeps reciting this prayer. My brain doesn't believe in God most of the time, but my prayer is 1M155U + my brain can say it 4ever.

That is school. There is nothing more 2 say about it. My hand is writing this in 6th period study hall, but there is nothing 2 say. School is a D place + so is home.

Maybe there will be more 2 write later.

432WP

After school 543 swamped me w/jobs, even though every 1 else was watching TV. Somehow Roger + Rebecca always get their work done without my eyes seeing them. My brain thinks 543 does it 4 them. They also had a snack 2day. After school my eyes saw 4 glasses (1 4 Emma + 1 4 Roxie) sitting in the kitchen sink. Each 1 had juice rings on the bottom.

ME: Is there any juice?

SOME OF US are not allowed 2 have anything after school except water, unless 543 feels like it.

543: NO WERE GOING 2 HAVE DINNER SOON.

Then my mouth said: But everybody else had some.

Sometimes my mouth interrupts.

543: NO THEY DIDNT.

My mouth said: Whose glasses are those?

My eyes were looking at the 1s in the sink + 543 knew it. 543 was lying 2 me.

543: YOUD BETTER DO YOUR CHORES + GET IN2 YOUR ROOM.

It was time 2 clean the kids' bathroom. This is always my job everyday, 543 hasn't cleaned 1 bathroom since THEY got married. The sink, the toilet, the tub, the floor. Sponge, scrubber, vacuum, mop. 543 checks, so IT IS DONE RIGHT. It reminds me of Cinderella, only no mice are helping me.

No GD mice.

(Does it bother U if my hand writes a word like that? Don't be upset, but my hand can't stop itself. If it bothers U, U would never want 2 know what my brain is thinking on the inside, the inside that can never come out.)

ME: Finished.

My brain was hoping 543 would let me watch cartoons w/Emma + the 3Rs.

543: YOU KNOW THE RULE, IN2 YOUR ROOM. YOULL BE CALLED WHEN YOUR DINNERS READY.

543 said: + DO YOUR HOMEWORK. YOU NEED 2 DO SOMETHING ABOUT YOUR GRADES.

Then my mouth said: Why doesn't everybody else have 2 do their homework?

543: THEY DONT NEED 2 WORK AS HARD AS YOU DO.

My mouth: But why?

543: GET GOING.

543 thinks that my brain is stupid.

Back in my GB, my hand locked the door + shut it. Could U tell how easy my hand wrote that? The words streamed out of my pen (it didn't mind). My hand has never written this be4. Now it is telling U.

MY HAND LOCKED MY DOOR + SHUT IT.

Do U remember about my GB? Do U remember where the lock is? It's an outside door. My hand locked my body out of the house. From 400WP 2 dinner time every day M-F (after bathroom cleaning), the door is supposed 2 be locked w/me in my GB. It was the same in every other house. They would put an outside lock on my room.

4 a long time my brain stopped thinking about it. My hand just turned the lock + did it. Being alone was OK. But my cheeks + my throat don't like it anymore + my hand doesn't want 2 lock the door.

It started w/the nowhere dream. My brain got the idea that there is a letter from U waiting 4 me but it'll never be delivered 2 my GB.

IT MUST BE FOUND.

So it tries 2 ignore the rule some days. Last wk, my hand just closed the door, didn't lock it. When 543 walked by + saw it unlocked, 543 locked it. That's why 2day my hand locked the door again.

My ears don't want 2 hear HER picky sticky little fingers clicking that lock.

Now Roxie just unlocked the door + opened it.

Dinner, she said.

Time 2 hide my NB + eat.

607WP

1M so M my hand can hardly make the pen move.

But 1M going 2 help.

1M going 2 write U everything.

So U will start 2 know.

At the table my dinner was freezing. 543 was M at me probably because of the juice + because it took a few min 2 finish writing 2 U in my NB after Roxie unlocked the door.

543: JULIE-ANN! NOW!

1M not Julie Ann.

14AT3 Julie Ann.

543 says it like it's a girl's name: Julie Ann.

1M Julian. Jool-yun — + 543 knows it. 543 is

Emma + the 3Rs were almost done by then, so 543 must have waited 2 let me out of the room anyway. My hamburger was burned + tasted like cold leather. The pinto beans came from a can + weren't even lukewarm + dessert was a chocolate-covered cherry, except mine was dented on the bottom, like some 1 had looked inside. But my mouth never got the chance 2 eat more than 2 bites of that crusty rusty charcoaly (charcoldy) hamburger, because my mouth said something.

My mouth is hard 2 understand. It knows it'll get me in trouble by talking, but my insides were D. My mouth was full of words. Isn't my body worth a hot meal, a better hamburger? Didn't my chores get done without any juice?

It was either yell

or C

or maybe D.

So my mouth yelled.

It said: This is the worst supper. It tastes like

My head acted like a turtle head pulling itself back inside because some maniac was about 2 chop it off w/a butcher knife + use it 4 turtle soup.

But no 1 was there. 543 was just standing in the kitchen making dinner 4 THEM. Steak.

Then 543 started humming.

My head was waiting 4 the ax.

543 just hummed louder + started la-la-ing.

But 43 charged in. 43 was back in their bedroom when my mouth started. 43 never eats w/us — only w/543 after we're done because maybe THEY think

THEY would get germs from being w/us.

43 rushed over 2 me.

43: DO YOU WANT THIS?

43 was M because the pipe in 43s hand was shaking. My eyes watched 43s hand in case 43 moved 2 hit me.

43: DO YOU WANT THIS?

ME: No.

Then 43 took my plate, walked 2 the garbage can + whacked it against the inside of the can. The whole dinner slid off in2 the plastic bag.

43: GET 2 YOUR ROOM NOW + NO MORE BACKTALK.

So my body went back 2 my GB like it's some kind of jail.

It is, U know.

A jail.

719WP

Some 1 just locked the door. Maybe it was 543. No 1 ever locked me in anywhere be4 543, + 43 doesn't care. 43 locks the door 2.

2 OLD 2 BE LOCKED IN MY ROOM.

NO 1 SHOULD BE LOCKED IN THEIR ROOM.

My eyes are C now because

732WP

Roger just came in 2 get something. He looked at me but didn't say anything. Now he's gone + my ears hear him locking the door. My hands want 2 K177 him.

My hands want 2 R this NB up. My hands want 2 R THEM up + throw the pieces away.

807WP

170V3 3MMA

Emma plays w/me when 543 lets her. We play dolls. Or school. Emma is 5 now.

Playing w/Emma is fun. She pretends 2 be Sleeping Beauty. She hides from the bad witch. Then she pricks her finger. Her prince (me) fights the dragon + rescues her. Sometimes 1K155 her. 543 would be M.

Emma doesn't remember WV. She was only 20 mo old when we left. She doesn't remember U (my brain thinks) either.

170V3 3MMA

Wish #1: that everything was fine, that 2 crazy people weren't in charge of me, that all of me was 4A99Y (really 4A99Y).

Wish #2: that U were here 2 help me. Ha, ha! If U were here, there wouldn't be a problem. If U were here . . .

Wish #3: that we were still in WV. At least that way we'd get 2 be close. 14AT3 being this far.

Wish #4: 1W154

1M wishing

1M

wishing

U could write 2 me.

170V3U

WN16
631 WA

All night 1M awake.

Everything's in my brain + all mixed up. What is happening 2 me? My eyes just read everything in my NB from the beginning + everything sounds crazy like it's all made up. But it's not. My brain only thought about this stuff, never let my hand write it. Now that it's staring back at me, my insides feel sick. Really sick.

It's early + Roger is still sleeping + 1M writing at my D. My pen is ready 2 work hard.

When 543 1st came, 543 4AT3D me right away. My face tried 2 look 4A99Y, but my eyes looked 5AD. 543 acted like Emma was HERS. 543 always treated 2Rs + Emma better or gave them more + 43 let 543 get away w/it + that bothers me most.

The 1st time 543 locked me in my room was 1 wk after 543 + 43 were married. We were still in WV + 543 made brussels sprouts 4 dinner. Emma was 2 little 2 try them but not me. BS were something new 2 me + my mouth didn't like them. 43 was out of town + 543 told me EAT THEM OR YOULL GO 2 BED W/O DINNER.

My eyes watched Roger put the BS in his napkin + then say he had 2 go 2 the bathroom. When he came back, they were gone. He dumped them down the toilet. But 543 didn't care, 543s eyes weren't watching him. All 543 wanted was me. 543 was going 2 get me.

543: EAT THEM UP JULIE ANN OR YOU CAN MARCH YOURSELF RIGHT UP 2 BED!

My mouth started 2 argue. It was just BS. Why

should anyone have 2 go 2 bed because of BS?

543 yelled at me + told me 2 go upstairs.

My mouth: NO!

So 543 got 1 of 43s belts + swung it so hard against the kitchen wall that the wallpaper ripped off the corner + the toaster hummed.

543: UPSTAIRS.

My feet moved me upstairs. There wasn't a lock on my door, but 543 locked it anyway. 543 put a rope around the doorknob + tied it 2 the banister. My brain didn't know at 1st, but when my hand tried 2 open the door, it was easy 2 figure out. My body turned into a wild animal that had been caught + put in a zoo. My mouth screamed, my hands pounded on the wall, my eyes C 4 a long time.

When it was time 2 P, 543 still wouldn't open the door so my bed was P'd. Just 2 serve 543 right.

Only 543 had a fit in the morning. 543 told me that those wet sheets would stay on my bed until my lesson was learned. Then at breakfast there was a glass of P on the table in my place.

DRINK IT ALL UP, 543 said.

My eyes couldn't tell it was apple juice. It just looked like P + my mouth wouldn't drink it. 543 picked it up + tried 2 make me. My eyes were C +

my mouth was screaming 4 543 2 stop. So 543 threw it on me. That's when my nose could smell the apple juice smell.

My feet ran upstairs + my body stayed in my room all morning. Then 543 knocked on the door.

YOUR LUNCH IS READY JULIE ANN.

My brain knew 543 was lying, but my mouth was 2 hungry 2 care. On the table was my lunch. A grilled cheese sandwich. An apple. A glass of milk.

BET YOURE HUNGRY, 543 said.

My eyes looked at that grilled cheese sandwich. It looked good. But my brain wondered if it had a mousetrap inside. If my hands picked it up, WHAP!

My eyes looked at it closer. Everything was all right. That's when my brain knew. 43 was coming home. 543 wanted him 2 think that everything was fine, that the problem was mine. The lunch looked fine. The wallpaper rip was fixed w/glue. The rope that tied my door closed was gone.

So when 43 came home a while later, my mouth tried 2 tell everything. Only 543 had told 43 1st. How Julie Ann had disobeyed 543, how Julie Ann hadn't eaten, how Julie Ann had yelled + C + carried on.

My mouth told 43: 543 treats me like a dog. Nobody ever did that be4.

43: JUST SHUT YOUR TRAP. YOU BETTER LEARN 2 GET ALONG W/543. THATS ALL THERE IS 2 IT.

My mouth: But

43: THERE ARE NO BUTS. YOULL LEARN 2 DO WHAT 543 SAYS.

Do U want 2 know how THEY began? 43 went out w/543 the 1st time on the night of the Miss America pageant. Why does my brain remember that? Why does my brain remember sitting there w/Pam English, my babysitter? Why does my brain remember the Miss America from Texas w/the blond hair?

Then 43 walked in w/543.

Get 2 bed, 43 said.

543 looked at me like 543 was wearing a mask + didn't want 2 crack it w/a smile. 543 stayed all night. My eyes saw them leave at 602WA. My ears heard the front door bang shut. 43 took 543 home. 43 left me alone w/Emma. 43 didn't see me peering through gauzy curtains.

That wk we visited 543s house. It wasn't a house, it was an old carriage house behind a mansion on National Road. There were naked light bulbs hanging from the ceiling + peeling wallpaper + cats running around. Rebecca + Roger were there. They slept in the same bedroom.

543 offered me some Coke, but when 543 poured it in a glass, my lips didn't want 2 touch it. My eyes saw things on the glass. My nose smelled dirt + cat P. The rooms were yellow or green. They felt cloudy + blurry. My eyes couldn't see straight in that garage. My brain needed some outside air.

The next day 43 asked me, How would U like 2 have XXXXXXXXXXXXXXXXX? There are words my hand can't write, sounds my mouth can't say. Is that weird? It's been that way 4 over 4 yr now. My brain can barely even think them. If it thinks them once, they sound like the loudest fire alarm in my head. My brain thinks them + it wants 2 pass out. My ears cannot listen 2 them, my mouth cannot answer any questions about them. My mouth doesn't want 2 say them at all, except my hand can write that they are:

XXXXXX
XXXXXXXXXX
XXXXX
XXXX

But my brain says CROSS THEM OUT NOW.

These words are driving me crazy especially the 1st 1. XXXXXX, XXXXXX, XXXXXX, XXXXXX. That's why my hand writes code words. Because it doesn't want 2 write bad words, hard words.

It didn't matter what my mouth said when 43 asked. 3 wks later 43 married 543. So my mouth kept shut. Roger + Rebecca moved in be4 the wedding. Roger brought his stuff right in 2 my room, no 1 even asked me.

THEY got married in the pastor's study at the Presbyterian Church on Edgington Lane. 43 never went 2 church on Sunday. They went away 4 a weekend + Pam English came 2 stay. Then they came back + 543 started w/BS + succotash + creamed spinach + eggplant every time 43 went out of town.

543 was pregnant w/Roxie. My fingers have counted it out many times. 543 got pregnant be4 543 got married. My fingers know. 543 said Roxie came out early, but my fingers know she didn't. 543 had her the month after we got 2 Tucson.

Be4 we left my ears heard people whispering everywhere. 43, 543, the neighbors put me in a whisper world. That's why 43 didn't tell anyone we were leaving. That's why we just packed up 1 day + left. At 202WA.

At least my eyes got 2 see U 1 last time be4 we went away. My bike took me 2 U 4 2 hr. Did U know? My mouth asked U 2 help me, but U couldn't.

My eyes were C like a fool.

732WP

2day things seemed better. 543 was almost friendly this morning + my bowl had almost as much cereal as Roger's. My eyes look at the cereal bowls every morning. Mine always has less. Sometimes a lot less, sometimes only a little. 543 puts the milk on it 2 so we won't use 2 much. When 543 is M at me 543 puts the milk on and lets it sit 15 min be4 calling me.

2day my cereal wasn't 2 soggy. It was probably enough that 543 locked me in all night. 543 was SMILING, but it won't last.

My hand wants 2 write about money 2day + how it wants some. THERE IS NO ALLOWANCE 4 ME. THEY say THEY can't afford it. But Roger gets money. Roxie gets money. THEY only give me 20c every school day 4 milk at school. THERE IS ONLY MM (MILK MONEY) 4 ME. BUT THERE IS MONEY:

THEM	3Rs + EMMA	ME
tequila	snacks + juice	MM
steak		
potato chips + dip		

If 1N33D 2 buy something (which is all of the time), MM MUST BE SAVED + there is only water 2 drink. Like for Ur NB, my mouth didn't drink milk 4 the 1st 7 days at UHS (it cost $1.27 w/tax + my hand got 13c change).

Every wk, my brain thinks about getting another $ of MM. That's what a wk of school is good 4. There are 36 wks every yr, so there is $36. What if it came all at once?

Some kids at school spend 2 or 3 $ a day at the cafeteria + snack bar: burritos, potato chips, apples, ice cream sandwiches, yogurt. Russell Bridges brings a bottle of Perrier every day, plus he stops at a store + buys a huge sandwich on the way 2 school. His parents just bought him a new car. Do U know how much a car costs? More than 2 lifetimes of MM 4 a cheap car. More than 4 lifetimes of MM 4 an OK car.

There is no car 4 me. There is only water from the water fountain + lunch (if U can call it that) out of my brown paper bag. Then the bag MUST be folded up + taken home 2 use again. Don't throw it out or 543 has a fit. 543 says they cost 2 much money 2 buy. Once when my brain 4got, 543 put my lunch in a big brown grocery store bag the next day. My mouth screamed + my eyes C + my hands threw it away be4 my body got 2 school; no 1 at school would understand. 1N33D 2 be like Russell Bridges. He probably doesn't even wear his (non-Kmart) underwear 2×s.

Sometimes my stomach is hungry, but mostly my brain ignores it + thinks about having more than my $1 MM. 1M going 2 be 16 next wk + then 1M getting a job. 1N33D 2 buy clothes + shoes (not from Kmart) + a car. Then maybe it will be time 2 RA RA RA RA RA.

Sometimes my brain is so unhappy it doesn't know what 2 do at all. My body sits in my GB + my brain wishes me D. Would the police investigate? My brain says no. THEY don't leave marks. THEY don't B me w/cigarettes, THEY don't S me in the bathtub with boiling water, H me w/electric cord, or T me up in a plastic bag. Those kids are in the newspaper. But all U have 2 do is look at my face + U can see it. If U know what you're looking 4. My eyes see it when they look at myself in the mirror. It is hard 2 look 4 long.

My mouth could turn THEM in. My brain has

memorized the hotline number. My eyes saw it in the paper once. But every 1 else (even Emma) is OK. THEY treat her OK + no 1 would believe me. Sometimes 1N33D 2 K177 THEM, 2 find a G somewhere + S THEM. But it would be jail 4ever + then Emma would be gone 4ever.

Sometimes my eyes read the food ads on Wednesday (that's the only day 543 buys the paper) + look 4 sales. If something is cheap + there is extra MM, the food is bought + stays under my B or in my D. 1M like a little pack rat, only 1M a snack rat. But so is Roger, only he's a robber. So MM only buys small things that can hide under other things and don't rattle or smell. Candy w/o wrapping paper is the BEST.

1 time my eyes saw a $5 bill on the sidewalk. My eyes made circles looking 4 traps. My brain made my foot step on it thinking it's better 2 lose my foot than my hand. But nothing grabbed it. So my hand bent down + picked it up.

The $5 bought food 2 eat right then. It bought a can of sardines (because it didn't need an opener). It bought 2 doughnuts + a bottle of Perrier + a big Hershey's candy bar. My mouth 8 it all, every bit. Like it hadn't eaten 4 yr. There was even a little money left over.

Tonight 543 made pancakes. It was like 543s test 4 me. Mine were cold + the test was: what would my mouth say? Would it scream + complain? Or would it just eat them + shut up. My hand is ashamed 2 write it, but my mouth was hungry + it wouldn't have cared if they were frozen. My mouth 8 them + didn't say 1 word.

1M wishing it didn't have 2.

TN17
735WP

My brain got really confused at school today.

MRS POPE (my English teacher) said she wanted 2 talk 2 me after school. My brain thought: probably something about all my Fs. But she didn't.

MRS POPE said, Your last paper was very good.

This was a puzzle. All my papers are usually Fs, but not this time. MRS POPE told us 2 describe someplace we knew very well. The only place my brain could think of was my GB + some of it could come from my NB 2 U.

Here is what was written just so U'll know.

My Bedroom

My bedroom is a cinder block cell shared w/5 baby lizards + 1 big Robber Reptile. Drather sleep w/the lizards.

The room used 2 be a carport + you can still see oil stains in the middle of the floor. It made a better carport.

There are 816 cinder blocks in my room. They are painted puke yellow. One light bulb hangs in the middle of the ceiling. It casts shadows on the wall, shadows that never move.

The closet is my favorite part of the room because it has a window that lets me look outside. When you have a room like mine, you want 2 look outside as much as you can. Except 4 being a quiet place, my room is not a place you want 2 stay 4 long. Especially when the Robber Reptile arrives.

But bars are on the window + a lock is on the door. A slot is at the bottom + food is shoved through it. No parole is possible, even 4 good behavior. Turning 18 is the only escape, but growing old takes 2 long. Sec move like hr on my watch.

My room feels like a place 2 stay 4ever. But my brain will invent a different watch + live by a different time.

1 day 1M going to be free.

MRS POPE said, you've got some talent there. Of course, you could abbreviate less + stop turning words into numbers. It's clever, but you don't want to break the rules all the time, do you? Anyway are you (maybe 1M wrong so don't misunderstand me) upset about something?

Somehow the idea flew into my head that she could read my brain. Like a witch or something.

MRS POPE said, Is something wrong?

All my brain could think about was 43 + 543 + the 3Rs. Then about U. 1M155U, 1M155U, 1M155U. Repeating repeating repeating that 2 myself

+ thinking about everything my mouth couldn't say.

MRS POPE said, Like school? Are you having a hard time adjusting 2 a new school? It can be difficult when you transfer.

Then my brain knew MRS POPE wasn't a witch at all. She didn't really know what was wrong.

ME: Guess so.

Then she touched my hand.

The last nice hand my brain remembers touching me was Urs.

MRS POPE said, Sometimes talking 2 someone can help. Don't shut everybody out. Why don't you talk 2 your counselor if you can't talk 2 me?

My mouth grinned like a deaf + dumb monkey.

MRS POPE said, 1M right down the street from you + see you walking by all the time. Have you seen me taking my baby 4 a walk? My eyes have seen her. They see everything about the neighborhood. My brain has memorized every crack in the sidewalk between my house + the corner by school. My brain knows how many ocotillos are planted on the left side (19, unless you count the dead ones, then it's 23). My brain knows which direction the irrigation canal runs (SE). My ears heard that MRS POPE was divorced (543 told me) +

has 4 kids. They remind me of the 3Rs, Emma, + me when we have 2 go someplace together. There's too many of them and they look like they want to cut loose and RUN. She doesn't have much money, you can tell. 543 said about her kids: THEY ARENT WELL DRESSED BUT AT LEAST THEYRE CLEAN.

Then MRS POPE said, Maybe you can come out + say hello some time. Teachers aren't that awful you know.

1M155U1M155U1M155U1M155U

MRS POPE: Where did you move from?

ME: Tucson.

MRS POPE: Did your F get relocated?

ME: Not really.

Then she asked 1 of THOSE QUESTIONS: What does XXXXXXXXXXX about Tempe?

My head started 2 buzz. My hands were shivering.

Time to go

going

gone

Julian

Friday November 18
409 WP

My brain thought about abbreviations + numbers 2day — TOday. Why 1 write them. Why EYE write them. Why I I I RITE them.

14AT3I.

14AT3I!

My hand tries not to use it. It looks NAKED. It sounds NAKED. My hand tries to stay dressed. But that's not the way that people write.

+ my hand wants to write.

ABBREVs + NOs: 170V3them. THEY don't sound like words. THEY don't look like words. THEY sound + look like secret code. THEY don't scare me or my pen.

ABBREVs + NOs: 170V3them.

Maybe ~~1~~ I will try.

My brain thought about Emma today. My eyes watched her (from the bathroom window) playing with 3Rs in the back yard after school. She has long light brown hair. She was smiling. She was laughing + jumping + playing like nothing was wrong.

Nothing was wrong

4 her.

Nothing was wrong.

Only 4 me.

Sometimes my brain thinks about RA. Do U know what it means? When my insides are very 5AD. But when my eyes see Emma RA is impossible. Sometimes my brain says: RA RA RA RA RA RA. Now Now Now.

Emma's face says:

No.

Saturday, November 19
816 WA

Something strange happened last night. THEY went out. They don't do that very often but it was some party for 43s new company. They left us home alone. Emma + Roxie went to bed at 800 WP, then Roger + Rebecca sat around watching TV with me. My eyes were looking through the TV section when they saw a listing for a late movie that started at midnight.

At 1100 WP Rebecca said, TIME TO GO TO BED. She sounds just like 543 when she gets bossy.

1M — I AM THE OLDEST ONE, but Rebecca gets to be the BOSS. She would tell on me if my mouth said anything, so I pretended. I went to GB with Roger. Only not to go to sleep. Roger turned out the light + my body made sleeping sounds. But my brain was counting to 60 slowly, 45 times. There is no clock in my GB + my W doesn't glow in the dark. But my brain knows how to count like a computer so it wasn't hard to keep counting. It was like a game + it was an easy game to win.

My brain counted to 60 + my fingers kept track of the 1s + the 4 corners of the room were the 10s, 20s, 30s, + 40s. The ceiling was the 50s. Then my brain started over. Does that make sense? That's just how my brain counts time out.

When my brain got to 45 × 60 it was 1155 WP so it must have counted a little too slow. But Roger was asleep. Rebecca was, too.

My fingers turned on the TV very low + my body sat right in front of it. My ears had to listen to see if THEY came home because THEYD K177 me if they saw me.

The name of the movie was 90J. It was an old movie starring old B+W people. It is hard to remember too well because my eyes had to watch while my ears were listening to the sound of cars. It was about a painter who meets a little girl. Only maybe she's not real because she disappears. But he meets her again — only she's older + more like a girlfriend. Then he finds out that she's from the past. She's been traveling to see him, to help him. He paints her picture + falls in love with her. Only he finds out what happened to her a long time ago + he realizes she's like a ghost. She must have appeared to HIM because they were meant for each other. He figures out how to be with her — only that's when THEY came home. My ears heard an engine. My eyes saw the headlights flash through the living room curtains as they pulled into the driveway.

My fingers turned off the TV + my feet ran down the hall. My heart was beating so fast. My brain wondered if they would stop + feel the top of the TV to see if it was warm. Then they'd know. But nothing happened except

My brain keeps hearing the tune in my mind. Only it can't remember the words. It's playing in my head right now. It's almost like the song is familiar. But the strange thing wasn't only the movie or the song.

I HAD MY NOWHERE DREAM AGAIN.

My NOWHERE DREAM is why I started this NB.

I was going crazy. I had to do something. So I started writing + my nowhere dream stopped.

Until last night.

The dream came back. There was a book with a letter in it. The letter is from U. In my dream my eyes can't read any of the words, but it is from U. The book is in an old place, maybe a library, + the letter is old. There is a letter waiting for me. Somewhere.

It makes me want to be like 90J. The girl kept appearing to the painter in the future. (Can U do that?)

Right now my brain is thinking about RA + I would if Emma weren't here. What would they do to her?

WISH:

I wish I could paint. I could paint Ur picture. I have no picture of U. Just the picture in my mind. I can only paint with words + they feel funny (+ NAKED). How can I SAY what U look like? How can I SAY how Ur skin felt? How can I SAY anything about U?

212 WP

Outside in the back yard: They said they were going out + who wanted to come. Everybody wanted to go except me. So 543 said: GET YOUR JACKET + GET OUTSIDE. THATS THE RULE.

ME: But it's cold today.

It is 57 today which is warm in WV but cold in Tempe.

543: BETTER GET GOING JULIE ANN.

My hands wanted to K177 543 when 543 said that. But instead they grabbed my jacket + NB + a couple of books to go outside. My ears heard 543 lock the back door. Then 543 checked my GB window. My fingers used to unlock it so I could sneak inside my room, but they caught me.

It just proved that I AM A LIAR + A THIEF. So now 543 always makes sure that the window is locked tight. A few min later, they all drove away. I walked around the house + checked the doors to see if they left one unlocked, but 543 is too smart for that.

Then I headed for a corner of the back yard where there's an old playhouse. Somebody built it a long time ago out of good lumber so even though it's falling apart, it's held up longer than most things would. At least I'm out of the wind. That's where I am now. Sitting in this playhouse writing U. Sometimes I feel like this is my real house. Whenever they go away + I stay home, I get locked outside.

THEY DONT TRUST ME. 43 says: YOU HAVE TO DO WHAT 543 SAYS. Do U know what that's like? My brain never used to care. But now it says: Why? My brain doesn't want to, my mouth wants to say NO! But it'll only get worse if my mouth starts screaming.

Then a girl walked into the back yard. She was wearing a white dress + had braids.

She stood in the door of the playhouse + said: This was my playhouse. I used to live here.

She had freckles + a smile + she seemed to be about 10. I knew her name. It was the girl from the movie.

ME: Why are you here?

J: To help you.

ME: How?

J: With 543.

ME: You mean — ?

J: You know who I mean. 543. 543 is trying to hurt you.

ME: But I don't let 543.

J: But 543 already has, + you don't know how much. I'm here to help you do something.

ME: What? K177 her?

J: You can't fight a witch + win. You have to wait for 543 to make a mistake + then you RA.

ME: Can I write a story about you + your braids + your white dress + your freckles?

J: I have to leave now. Goodbye.

She ran out of the playhouse + when I looked outside, no one was there.

Did you like my play? Maybe I will write plays when I grow up. I'm leaving now, too. Bye.

802 WP

Now I'm sitting at my GB D. After writing to U this afternoon I went to the university library. Arizona State isn't too far away, right down University Dr. Sometimes I go there just to walk around + wonder what it would be like to be there, on my own. Sometimes I go to the library + walk up + down the stacks of books, kind of browsing.

Today I went to the computer catalog + typed 90J to see if maybe it was a book + it was! The author is Robert Nathan. I found it on the third floor. They had 1 copy, so old it looked like it was ready to fall apart. I sat down at a table + started to read it. When I got to page 13 (my lucky number?), I found the words to the song that the little girl sings in the movie.

Where I come from
Nobody knows;
Where I am going
Everything goes.
The wind blows
The sea flows —
And nobody knows.

I memorized them by H. I wanted to keep reading, but there was NO TIME. It was getting too late. I decided to come back next weekend, so I hid the book in a special place. Just for (SELFISH) me. I want to finish the book + I want to see the movie again. I want to know how everything ENDS.

My brain remembered the last time my eyes saw U, how U pulled me close + squeezed me as hard as U could (which wasn't very hard at all), + my nose smelled the baby powder + the warm smell of U. U kissed me + U were C, but my eyes wouldn't. They thought they would be able to see U again.

Only they never did.

Afterwards I walked around. I 4AT3 downtown Tempe. It's all new brick buildings trying to look like old brick buildings. They're filled with college food + designer clothes + cookies. Acuras, Celicas, RICH

KIDS with permanent tans + black sunglasses. College guys with GIRLFRIENDS. I can't walk there very often because my eyes see things they want. So I go the other way where it's safer to look.

By the time I got home, it was 532 WP + my brain thought they would wonder where I'd been + be M. But they weren't even home. So I sat in the playhouse + waited. Every time my ears heard a car drive down the street, my brain thought it was them. My eyes would see the headlights around the front of the house, but my ears kept waiting to hear 4 doors slamming.

They didn't slam until 705 WP. It was dark + cold.

I said, what's for dinner?

They were still getting out of the car.

ROGER (creep): We had dinner already.

He can be a real liar sometimes so I tried not to believe him.

REBECCA: We went to Red Lobster.

ROGER: I had the shrimp platter.

My eyes looked at 543 then and my mouth said: Everybody had dinner?

Emma said, I had fish fingers. She was smiling at me like she was proud of herself. Didn't she understand?

543: EVERYBODY EXCEPT YOU. BUT THATS WHAT YOU GET WHEN YOU STAY HOME BY YOURSELF.

ME: Well, I'm starving —

543 (sounding so sweet): ILL FIX YOU SOMETHING.

543 fixed me something all right: 543 took 2 pieces of Wonder bread + a thin piece of reject bologna + a knifeful of French's mustard + made a sandwich for me. Then 543 counted out 8 Doritos + put them on a napkin.

543: GET YOURSELF A GLASS OF KOOLAID + THATS DINNER.

My hands wanted to take that sandwich + S it into 543s face. My hands wanted to T that Koolaid all over 543. My mouth could eat 10 sandwiches. Do you know how much my body weighs? 115. I'm almost 5 ft 10. My brain doesn't think I'm going to die from starvation (do U know?), but I know it wouldn't hurt 543s feelings if I did.

I am C
Not just about stupid THEM
About us.
About
U
dear
XXXXX

Monday, November 21
505 WP

I am feeling sort of 4A99Y.

Sort of

4A99Y.

I'm afraid to be 4A99Y. Why? Because I'm afraid something bad will happen. But that's silly.

OK,IMHAPPY. I don't feel that way very much. I can't believe what happened either.

MRS POPE gave me an A on my GB paper. She wrote: This is good work, Julian. Thank you for sharing your special place with me.

+ S just called. I was out raking gravel in the front of the house + 543 wouldn't call me in.

543: YOU USE THE PHONE TOO MUCH. YOURE ALWAYS CALLING THE TIME. WHAT DO YOU CARE WHAT TIME IT IS? YOURE NOT GOING ANYPLACE.

543 is wrong. I can check the time if I want to, I just want to make sure my W is working. 543 knows that.

S said she would call back. Why would S call me? She hardly ever says anything to me at school except HERE when she hands me something or THANKS when I hand her something. Should I tell U her name now? I guess it doesn't matter. It's Susan.

732 PM

They ruined it just like they ruin everything. EVERYTHING! I was in the kitchen doing the dishes when the phone rang. 543 grabbed it.

543: WHO DO YOU WANT? WHO? WHO?

Wishing it was a wrong number.

543: OH, YOU MUST MEAN JULIE ANN. HES DOING DISHES NOW.

Running for the phone.

543: YOU MUST BE IN ONE OF JULIE ANNS CLASSES. DID YOU CALL HIM BEFORE?

Grabbing the phone + 543 let go.

543: 3 MIN. DONT FORGET. IM TIMING. ITS ALREADY 255.

ME: Hello?

S: Hi, it's Susan. From Spanish?

543: 250 SO TALK FAST.

S: Julian?

My eyes watched 543 walk away. 10 steps + 543 was out of the kitchen.

S: Are you there?

ME: Uh huh.

S: Are you OK?

Now my mouth didn't want to talk about being OK, about being any THING.

ME: Uh huh.

S: You weren't saying anything.

543 was waiting around the corner in the hall. My ears could hear 543 listening. No one else would know 543 was there but me.

S: I thought I'd call to see if you wanted to work on your dialog. After all, Mr. Thomas made us partners this time.

S stopped talking. She was skating on thin ice. I knew about the dialog partners + she knew it. We were supposed to work on our dialog in class, but I just sat there + wouldn't talk, so she started memorizing it herself.

S: You could come over to my house, if you want. I'm one street over.

Why was S being nice?

My mouth never talked to her, my eyes just watched the ends of her hair brushing against the top of my desk. Just the ribs in her white turtleneck where they outlined the back of her B.

S: You can come over now if you want. Or tomorrow after school.

543: 2 MIN.

ME: Can't.

Why not why not why not why not

S: OK, well, I thought I'd ask. It's my grade, too, you know. I thought maybe we could help each other out.

1M155U1M155U1M155U1M155U

S: You can let me know tomorrow if you change your mind.

Then she was gone + my insides felt all D. It was wrong to write that I was 4A99Y this afternoon. I can't be 4A99Y. It's not allowed.

543: WHAT DID SHE WANT?

I didn't want to tell 543 but I did.

543: WHAT KIND OF GIRL WOULD ASK A BOY OVER? ONLY ONE KIND THAT I KNOW.

ME: We're supposed to be partners on our dialog.

543: THATS WHAT YOU THINK + JUST IN CASE YOU GET ANY IDEAS ABOUT GOING, GO RIGHT AHEAD, BUT THE DOORLL BE LOCKED WHEN YOU GET BACK.

My hands wanted to T the phone at her + forget S called. But then 43 came home + I decided to tell about my A in English. I waited till 43 was done with dinner because I know how 43 hates to be interrupted. Out in the hallway my ears tried to listen for a good time but 543 kept talking to 43 kind of whispery like 543 was saying something bad. I walked in anyway + stood by the table. 543 kept whispering then it got real quiet.

ME: I got an A in English.

Down went 43s tequila glass + 43 said, Come here.

But my body was already too close. 43 grabbed onto both my hands + pulled me close enough to smell 43s mouth fumes.

Then 543 grabbed my arm + 43 let me go.

543: WHY DONT YOU TELL US ABOUT WHAT YOU STOLE? INSTEAD OF LYING. FOR A CHANGE.

ME: I didn't steal anything.

543s nails dug in.

543: COME HERE THIEF.

543 pulled me to the Forbidden Cupboard by the stove. I am not allowed to open it because this is where 543 keeps cookies, candy, potato chips, EVERY-THING, ALL THE GOOD STUFF 543 EATS OR DOLES OUT (secretly) TO THE 3Rs + tries not to give to me.

SOMETHINGS MISSING, 543 SAID, like 543 was singing a song.

ME: I didn't take anything.

543: JULIE ANN, YOU HAVE CHOCOLATE ON YOUR MOUTH.

543 made me feel like I had been dipped in chocolate.

ME: What chocolate?

543: CHOCOLATE CHIPS.

543 shoved the bag in front of my face.

ME: Why don't you ask Roger?

543: ROGER WOULDNT DO A THING LIKE THAT.

ME: He takes stuff all the time.

He was a Robber Reptile, but 543 didn't want to know that.

543: YOU CAN GO TO YOUR ROOM. YOULL BE LOCKED IN TONIGHT.

ME: But I didn't

43: Get to your room.

ME: I just wanted to go to

My eyes started C. I couldn't help it. I wish I could R my eyes out when I get started. Boys shouldn't C, MY BRAIN KNOWS THAT. It makes me a little girl or something. But my eyes can't help it.

So I came to my room + they locked the door + I started writing to U. It's almost 11 which means Roger is coming to bed + now they can unlock the door.

1047 WP

543 walked in + handed me a 2-lb can from Maxwell House Coffee.

543: DONT WANT YOU TO P ON THE FLOOR.

Then 543 took a pillow + blanket from Roger's bed + started to shut the door.

ME: Where's Roger?

543: HES SLEEPING ON THE LIVING ROOM COUCH. HE NEEDS TO STAY AWAY FROM YOU.

1M155U1M155U1M155U1M155U

ME: But I didn't do

Click

CLICK

CLICK!

That's all my ears heard. I am going out of my mind. Roger took the chips. I know he did. He does all kinds of stuff they don't know about. So he gets to sleep on the couch (and P on the couch). Maybe he'll steal something else tonight. But it probably won't matter because 543 will blame me anyway.

My eyes are staring at my P can.

This does not make sense.

My ears are still hearing the CLICK. My brain is thinking about it being a nighttime CLICK. This is worse than a daytime CLICK.

My hand can't write anymore tonight.

My brain is going crazy.

Tuesday, November 22
630 WA

Dear J,

I am writing the 1st letter of Ur name. I decided to be brave + not cross it out. I stayed awake all night thinking. Ss phone call makes me want to be braver.

What if we pretended?

What if ~~U~~ YOU were

I don't know if I can pretend about this.

What if YOU w

Why does my hand want to stop writing? Why does my brain want to blank out? Why do I want to start C?

I think a lot about how YOU could come here like 90J. YOU could come + find me. I am sending you messages, 1M155U1M155U1M155U1M155U. I don't pray at night, but I THINK of YOU. I tell YOU where I am, I ask YOU to rescue me, I hope that there was some mistake.

Sometimes I pretend that YOU are my girlfriend now. That's what I pretend when I write YOU in my NB. That's why I felt funny telling YOU about S. Would YOU be jealous? How could I have 2 girlfriends? Only, really, I don't have any girlfriends. Not YOU + not S.

Now I am not pretending. I remember sleeping with YOU before YOU left. I remember lying on the pillow next to YOU under a thousand blankets in the softest bed in the bedroom of the darkest nights.

I watched YOU sleep.

YOU weren't snoring, just breathing heavily. Not the deepest sleep. I wanted to wake YOU up + I blew on YOUR face. I saw the tiny light hairs above your upper lip move, + I felt bad that I was trying to wake

YOU up. But YOU weren't moving. YOU were very still, except for breathing. At least I could hear YOU breathing.

I wanted to stay there with YOU every night. I still dream of finding YOU there.

When I pretend.

Julian

NB #2:

The Junkman in McMop Land NB

Thursday, November 24
Thanksgiving
113 WP

43 stole YOU.

When I got home from school on Tuesday, I wanted to write about some things that had happened with Mrs. Pope, but YOU weren't there. I dumped out my desk drawer + I looked everywhere. I couldn't believe it, but YOU WERE GONE.

That's when 43 came in.

43: Looking for something?

43 had this sick little smile like some kind of pervert. I don't care if 43 reads this. 43 is a pervert + I ~~4AT3~~ HATE 43.

ME: I want my NB back.

43: You're sick + you're a liar. You're sick. What you wrote is sick.

43 is a lot sicker than me.

ME: I want my NB.

Then 43 laughed like I was crazy.

43: You won't get that back. Never. Maybe we'll have to send you away, if you ~~4AT3~~ HATE things so much. Then you won't have to put up with us. But wherever we sent you, you'd probably make them just as sick as you make us + they'd send you right back here again. You better take care of that sick mind of yours.

Then 43 shut the door but didn't lock it. As soon as I could, I walked out the back door + checked the garbage cans. I figured 43 might have thrown the NB out, but it wasn't there. I checked the kitchen garbage too, but it wasn't there either. Then I began to wonder if 43 hid it somewhere in

I HATE 543! 543 just pulled the door open + saw me writing.

543: Starting another NB full of lies? Is it about SOMEBODY I know? (I wanted to D. I turned up the page so 543 couldn't see.) You're such a hateful boy. No wonder you don't have any friends.

ME: I'm doing my homework.

543: You're a liar. You don't do your homework anymore. I wouldn't start another NB if I were you. We just might send you away.

Then 543 closed the door.

I HATE 543.

I don't know what to do. I want my NB back. I've got to hide this one. Or I've got to carry it with me all the time. Maybe I'll do that. Maybe I'll take it to school with me + tuck it into my jeans at home. Maybe they'll try to take it. I don't know.

I remember reading books about prisoners who decide to keep journals. They write on toilet paper, they write on their clothes, + no one finds out. This is like being in prison. DID YOU READ THAT? Prison is too nice a word for how I feel about this place.

I made 43 pay for it, too. I saw some change on 43s dresser yesterday morning + I took 35c to buy a new NB. Then I rode up to the Circle K to get one, only I had to buy a smaller one than last time. Because I didn't have enough money. I should've taken more. I don't care if 43 finds out that I took the money. What can 43 do to me? Give me less to eat? Lock me in my room? Send me to a reform school?

322 WP

I just ate dinner. It was a 49c turkey 543 got for shopping at Smittys. It tasted like a 49c turkey. I bet there aren't too many people eating 49c turkeys today.

We didn't eat 49c turkey in West Virginia. Or canned cranberry sauce or potato buds with freeze-dried gravy. Or Mrs. Smith's pumpkin pie. It's hard to even think about eating food, real food, again. Last year I read a book about a man who was sent to a Russian prison camp. He spent a lot of time describing the food he ate, except it wasn't really food, it was gruel. I know exactly what he went through, even if I'm not in Siberia. We are both in H.

Now I want to talk about Mrs. Pope. That's what I was going to tell YOU on Tuesday. That's when 43 was in my room.

Mrs. Pope asked who wanted to get extra credit. Nobody raised their hand, including me. I don't think anyone cares about extra credit. Most kids act like they don't want to be there at all. But after class, I told her I wanted extra credit. I will pass her class. I know it now + maybe I could get an A.

My brain thinks about Mrs. Pope more + more. Sometimes I think about telling her everything. When my brain thinks about her in its shadowy part, it thinks it can trust her. But when my eyes see her in person, standing in that classroom with the green linoleum + gray cinder block walls + BRIGHT white fluorescent lights, my brain knows it can't. There's no place to hide, no shadows, no darkness.

I can't trust anyone.

Except YOU.

After school Mrs. Pope said, How are things at home?

Part of me thought THIS IS YOUR CHANCE. Another part thought: SHUT UP + DONT SAY ANYTHING!

I didn't say much. Like, OK.

P: Sometimes, if you don't talk about something, it helps to write about it. Have you ever thought about keeping a journal?

I wondered if she was reading my mind again.

ME: No.

P: Or write a novel. Sometimes interesting things can come from a writer's imagination. Have you ever thought about that?

No.

P: You know, you're just what? 15? SE Hinton wrote The Outsiders when she was 16, I think. You could write a novel. You write well enough, you know. Have you ever thought that you could be a writer when you finish school?

No.

My head was pounding.

P: Why don't you try your hand at it? I'd be happy to read anything you wrote. That's a way you could get extra credit from me.

I was thinking a million things at once. I knew I had to say something, but WHAT WHAT WHAT?

I said: (I measured out each word like it was MM + said it to my brain before I said it to her. I was afraid I would tell her too much.) I like to write BUT

That's when I stopped. That BUT was too much. I didn't even know what I was going to say, but it was going to get me in trouble.

P: But what?

1M155U1M155U1M155U1M155U

P: I thought you were going to say something.

1M155U1M155U1M155U1M155U

P: Julian, you've got to do something about yourself. If you can't talk, you've got to write. Even if you don't show it to me.

I couldn't even look at her because her eyes were looking right at me + mine felt kind of funny.

ME: Goodbye.

Maybe I will write a novel.

Maybe I won't.

But always I will write to you.

Even if someone steals it.

Saturday, November 26
231 WP

Happy Birthday To Me! If I don't say it to myself, nobody will. This morning they were going out. To buy me a present? I wanted to think that they would, but I wasn't expecting one. Last year I got two pairs of socks + a 3-pack of underwear (all on sale).

From Kmart.

They asked me to go. I said I didn't want to. Which meant I'd have to be locked outside. I was ready for them. I knew 543 would check my SR window, so I made sure that I left the bathroom window open + the screen undone. 543 never noticed it, maybe because it's a small window. Only I'm so skinny I could climb through a drainpipe.

As soon as they were gone with the 3Rs, I climbed through the bathroom window + went straight to their bedroom. I hadn't forgotten what he took.

They have one deep closet with all kinds of things on the shelves. That's where I started. I felt funny, like they had booby-trapped everything so they'd know if it'd been touched. A thin wire stretched across the door like in James Bond movies. You can't see it, but when it's missing, the spy knows someone's been tampering with his property. Or a hidden camera taking my picture, beaming it to the dashboard TV of their Jaguar.

But I looked anyway. Shoeboxes filled with bills + tax stuff. Then there was one cardboard box tucked up on the highest shelf, way in the back. I knew my NB wasn't in it but I opened it anyway. I saw some old papers, bank books — all about West Virginia. Then I saw my name on one bank book. I remembered it. It was red + felt like leather + that's where I put all my Christmas + birthday money. It was my savings account for college.

I opened it:

BALANCE $0.00

The page was stamped: ACCOUNT CLOSED. I guess I wasn't surprised that they would steal my money, but it doesn't matter because 2 seconds later I found something more important.

A picture of you + me.

Julian +

YOU.

I don't know why 43 has it, but 43 doesn't have it anymore. I put it in my pocket right away. It's mine now. I am holding it in my left hand while I am writing. I won't let it go.

I put everything back in the closet + then checked the dressers. I found my NB under the clothes in his bottom drawer. 43 tried to hide it, but there it was. I wondered if I should take it right then. 43 wouldn't throw it out, I figured. If I took it then, 43 would know + I'd get killed. Now that I know where it is, I can keep checking on it + when the time's right, I'll get it back.

Then I snuck back outside + closed the window. They never noticed. I worried about nothing.

Everything is fine.

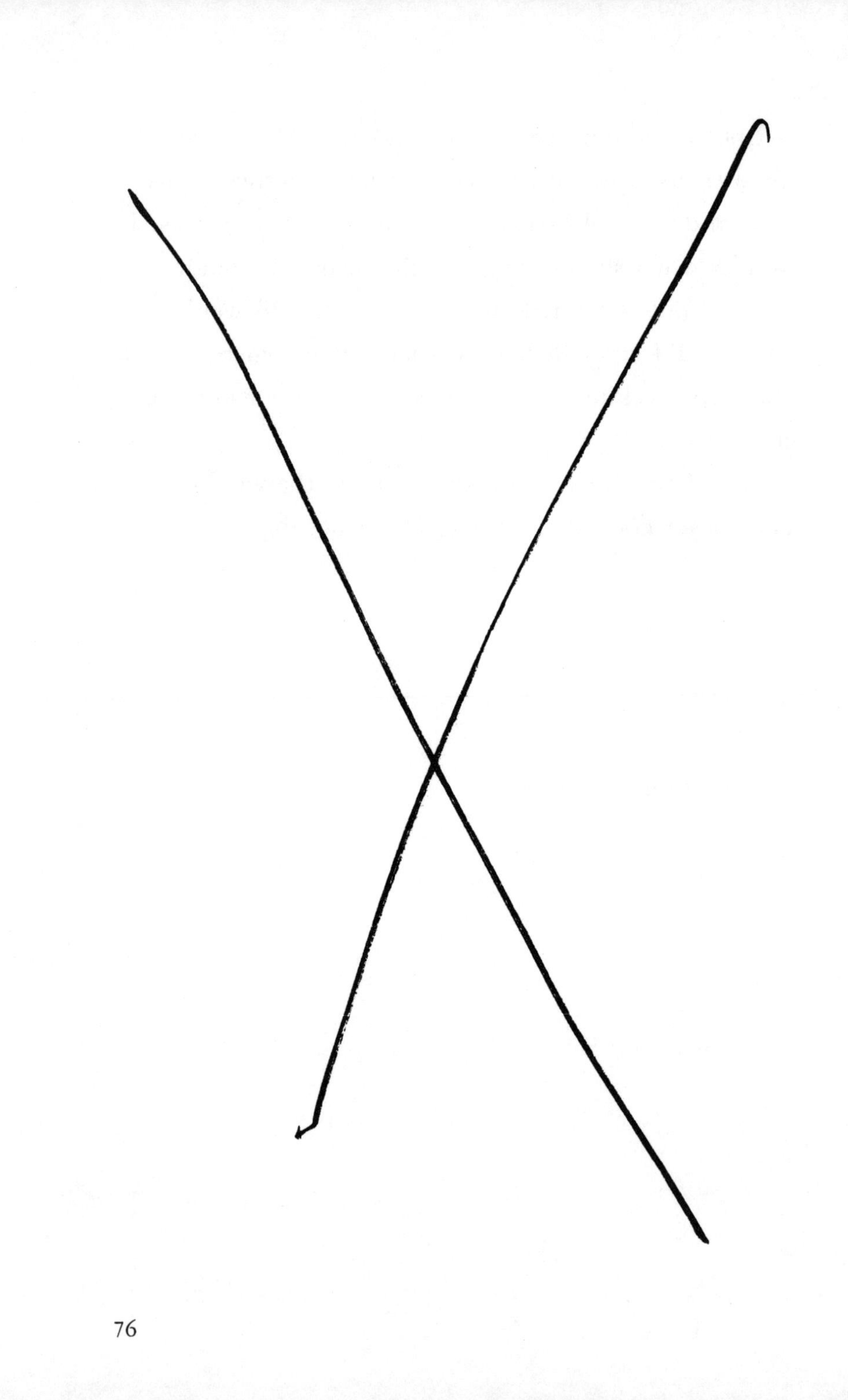

Everything.

I lied to YOU. Lying, lying that's all I'm doing. Your name is Jenny.

JENNY.

Jenny,

43, no not 43, he, HE found me in his bedroom. HE walked into the house + saw me.

I couldn't tell YOU. I couldn't tell myself. I hear the words in my head + I start C.

Jenny.

JENNY,

HE said, I knew you were going to try something like this.

HE was taking off his belt.

I said, I just want my NB.

HE said, Well, it's gone.

I had already shut the dresser drawer, so HE didn't know that I knew HE was lying.

HE wrapped the belt around HIS right hand like a bullwhip.

HE said, Bend over this bed.

1M155U1M155U1M155U1M155U

I mean it right now.

1M155U1M155U1M155U1M155U

+ HE swung the belt out + hit me hard on the arm. It felt like the sting of a giant hornet. A welt blew up on my arm like a red balloon. HE said, What you wrote in that NB was garbage. I told you you were sick + I meant it. I think you need a girlfriend. She's not your girlfriend. She's your GD XXXXXX.

M
if I write
        O
        1 letter at a time
                T
                I will spell
                        H
                        what he said

Only I can't put it all together. This is the worst word I know. The word that makes my brain disintegrate. A word that K1775. KILLS

JENNY

URMYM

UR

MY

M

My blood feels like hot liquid metal in some steel factory. Sparks are flying. Metal lava is flowing. I am not wearing protective clothing. I am worried that I will catch fire + D.

I will try to write it again.

U

R

MY

MOT

HER

NOT

HER

I don't want to finish the word.

I know you're not my girlfriend. I know.

Mah

Me

That's what I used to call you.

Before.

HE said, she's been D 4 years GDit.

I know that, too. I have thought about you Jenny every second every millisecond of those 4 years. I have dreamed about you. I have tried to picture you in my mind. Only now I have a real picture of you. I don't know why HE had it. HE took everything of yours + gave it away.

Do you know what HE did? Could you see?

The day after you D HE took everything of yours + threw it into boxes + dumped it on the grass by the street for the Wednesday garbage. Boxes of your clothes, your baby book, all of your books. I tried to save some things, but HE yelled. I mean HE YELLED, HE SCREAMED. HE said SHES D YOU GET AWAY FROM THERE. THATS D PERSON STUFF. I DONT WANT ANY D PERSON STUFF IN THIS HOUSE.

HE could have given it all away to Goodwill, but HE didn't. Instead, people came + picked through everything. Cars drove down the street + stopped. They always did that on Tues nights before the Wed garbage truck came. Families got out of their cars + picked through everything. You were broken into a million pieces + taken by a hundred people in lots of beat up cars. By Wed morning, nothing was left, except junk, torn paper, stained clothes. I thought people might miss some of your books. I tried to hide your favorites before HE YELLED, but someone found them. GONE WITH THE WIND + A NIGHT TO REMEMBER. Those two were your favorites. You wrote your name in them inside the cover. Jenny Sayre Drew. I can still see your name in them. I go to libraries + look for your favorite books + check to see if your name is inside the cover. It could be a coincidence, it could be like winning a billion-dollar lottery. I know stranger things have happened.

Haven't they?

I only saved one thing from the trash pickers. I have it with me all the time. It is your W.

Your Watch.

I hid it for a long time. I wasn't supposed to follow your time. NO ONE knew I had it. I put it in my shoes, in my pockets, under my mattress. I peeked at the time. I knew when it was WA + WP. I counted every second. I still do. Sometimes I think that the only thing that's mine is TIME, + it's your time too.

When I was 13 (do you want the exact day + time?) the band broke so I found a piece of heavy string + tied it to the watch + started wearing it around my neck. That kept it close to my H, my most private place of all.

Roger saw it then. They all looked at it. But they thought I found it in SOMEONES GARBAGE. HE (F) didn't remember what your watch looked like.

HE didn't even remember

YOU.

I thought about you every second HE whipped me with the belt. HE made me bend over + pull down my pants. HE didn't make me bleed. I've seen pictures of bleeding slaves. But there were hot red belt marks + my tears. All gone by the next morning.

For 4 years you've been D. JENNY. MOMMY. MOTHER. For 4 years I've had HER. SOMEBODY. STEPONHER.

STEPNOT-HER: I ~~4AT3~~ HATE that word. I want to STEP all over HER.

HE said: GET OUT OF HERE. I DONT WANT TO CATCH YOU IN HERE AGAIN.

STEPNOTHER was standing in the living room looking like SHE wished I had remote-control grenades buried in my brain + SHE had the detonator in her hand. YOU HAD NO BUSINESS IN THERE LIAR.

I just kept on walking out the door. The 3Rs +

Emma watched me from the car. I think Rebecca was smiling. Emma looked confused. I have to tell her what's going on. Now that she's 5 she can understand.

I have to tell her about YOU.

I sat on the side of the house by the pink oleander bush + tried not to C. I heard HER going through the house testing all the windows. I wasn't going to get in again. A few minutes later they slammed the door, got in the car, + drove away. I probably wouldn't get any dinner + I hadn't had lunch. I had exactly 17c so there wasn't much I could do.

I pulled out your picture + looked at it. I want to see you again. I want to be with you. Your picture made me feel good but it made me feel terrible too. It made me miss you too much, more than when I say 1M155U.

I thought about going to Mrs. Pope's house. Would she think I was crazy? I couldn't tell her anything about this. But I walked down the street to her house anyway.

Her kids were playing in the front. The oldest one, maybe 5, was pushing the baby in the stroller real fast, making wheelies on the driveway. The baby was squealing, real happy. The other kids were running around like they had a lot of excess energy. Maybe I could try.

ME: Is your M home?

She's inside, the oldest one said turning the stroller in circles.

The house looked dark. All the curtains were closed. I rang the doorbell + waited. Mrs. Pope answered the door.

She was wearing a nightgown. The hall behind her was dark and shadowy.

Julian? she said. I'm not dressed.

My feet wanted to leave. I needed clothes + bright lights.

Okay, I said + started to walk away.

Julian, no wait. Did you come to talk?

She stepped onto the carport.

She said, I'm sorry. I don't know what's wrong with me today. Can you come back later? All right? This afternoon some time? Maybe after three.

My feet stepped backwards.

She said, no really, I want you to promise me you'll come back. Please? I'll be here. I'll pull myself together by then. Okay? You promise? I can't not talk to my future SE Hinton.

So I went to the library. That's where I am now. I'm not sure what to do. I looked for 90J but it was gone. It wasn't in the special hiding place or on the right shelf. Who took it? WHO? SHE probably did. SHE ruins EVERYTHING!

I don't feel like reading 90J today anyway, it would just make my eyes want to C. I hate it so much, I can't stand being at home.

I would like to RA RA RA RA RA. But what about Emma?

Maybe she can RA too.

Sometimes I wonder what would happen if I DISAPPEARED. I've seen that on television. Sometimes a kid just disappears. Like he's the rabbit in a magic show. One day he's home, taking up space, the next day he's not. The parents say they can't figure out why their child disappeared.

But I don't believe the parents. I always know what's been happening at home. That kid's been getting killed, that kid's been getting burned hamburger, that kid has a P can in his bedroom, that kid has a lock on his door. That kid has a stepnother.

Maybe one day that kid will be me.

+ Emma.

Sometimes I think about being in other people's families. Maybe I'll see a family in their car + they're dressed nice + seem happy + I'll wonder what it would be like to be with them. Would they yell at me? Would they give me a P can + a locked door? Would I be happy with them?

Would they L me?

630 WP

It is getting dark + I'm sitting in the playhouse. I thought they'd be back by now, but they're not. They are probably eating steak at the Sizzler or something.

I didn't go back to see Mrs. Pope. After I left the library I went to Pic'n'Save to see what I could buy for 17c. I got 6 pieces of hard candy. They were 3c each, but what I like about Pic'n'Save is that they have a little bowl by the cash register for pennies. You can put yours in or take 1 or 2 if you need them, so I helped myself. The candy wasn't much, but it was better than nothing. Right?

Then I walked through the shopping center, past the bookstore + the pizza place. I was just trying to kill time. Then I was walking by the Tempe Antique Mart. It's just this small place. I never paid any attention to it, except today they had something in the window. A sunflower pitcher, just like the one you used to keep milk in, the one you got from Grandma's apartment when she D. It made me think about sitting at our old kitchen table, pouring milk on my cereal, eating breakfast with you. It made me think about you.

I wanted that pitcher.

How much is that? I asked the man in the store.

I figured the price was on the bottom, but I didn't want to touch it. I thought he might yell at me to get out. Some stores don't like kids around. But he didn't seem to care.

$65.

That's a lot, I said.

It's in good condition. I can let you have it for 60.

That's still a lot.

OK, 55.

I don't have that much money.

Well, there's some other pitchers back there that don't cost so much. You want to look around?

So I looked around. There was stuff everywhere. Tons of it. I started getting excited like

Like what?

Write it, Julian.

Like I was going to find YOU there.

I wanted to look through that store + find YOU. But how could you be in Arizona? I looked anyway.

There were old things like furniture + lamps + dishes + kitchen stuff. Lots of magazines. Toys. Postcards.

Then I got another idea. My eyes saw a sign that said WE BUY QUALITY GOODS.

I think you know most things about me now. Except one or two. Now I will tell you one of my secrets: I like to I like to go through things that people are throwing out. I do it almost every day, but Monday + Thursday are the 2 big days around here. Sometimes I dream about finding a mansion where the owners are throwing everything away. It gets my heart racing so much sometimes that I can't fall asleep at night.

So here's my next secret: I take the stuff home and make THINGS. I feel funny writing this, because I know what THEY think. SHE calls me RAGPICKER. He calls me SICK SICK SICK. + Roger tried to break my THINGS but even he gave up after a while.

I never made THINGS until after you went away. I started in Tucson. I found some postcards + wire + I made this THING. I never thought about making it. I just did. I started twisting the wire + adding the postcards + before I knew it, it was a THING. I put it on my wall. It stayed on my wall until we moved to HOUSE #2. Then it GOT LOST, but I know how. Everything I make gets lost when we move to a new house. So each time I start over.

Except now that I know about the Antique Mart, maybe I'll stop making THINGS. Maybe I can find stuff to sell. MONEY IS IMPT + MM ISN'T ENOUGH.

It is getting too dark to write. It's 715 WP. I can see a little bit from the streetlight, but not enough to keep writing unless I want to kill my eyes. I am getting cold, too.

Think about warm times, the girl says. Her name is Jennie. She is from 90J. I can tell you what that is now. PORTRAIT OF JENNIE. She is like you, only she spells her name differently.

She is standing here beside me. She says, Think about being at Myrtle Beach when you were little + got your sunburn.

I will, I am.

HOT

+

COLD

GOOSEBUMPS.

Sunday, November 27
1130 WA

They got home at 740 WP last night. I got one frozen waffle (barely toasted), apple butter on it (no syrup), a carrot (unpeeled), + an Oreo (chipped). Then they gave me another pack of underwear for my birthday + a pair of Keds (half price). They didn't even know if they were the right size. They just put them on my desk when I was in the bathroom. They didn't wrap them, or anything.

+ there wasn't any cake for dinner.

But Roger gave me another present this morning. THEY were in the back yard cutting back some oleander bushes, only the kids were inside. I walked back to my GB + saw Roger doing something in THEIR bedroom.

I looked at your watch: 1008 WA.

M: What're you doing?

R: I'll show you if you won't tell.

So I walked in + saw. In HER jewelry box, if you lift it up just right, there's a secret place underneath where you can keep money. SHE had a bunch of money there.

R: I just took a dollar. She buys us special snacks with this money sometimes.

M: But SHEll find out.

R: No, she won't. She doesn't count things the way you do. You can take a dollar too.

M: I don't want a dollar.

Then I thought: SHEll blame me for the missing dollar. I'll be the punished one. Roger will get away with it again. Unless I tell on him.

But how could I tell on him? He'd lie + she'd believe him. All I know is that I definitely saw 6 $20 bills, a $10, + 2 $5s. But I think there were more.

SHE could've bought me a birthday present with that.

If SHE wanted to.

SHE could've said Happy Birthday to me.

If SHE wanted to.

But no one else did either.

415 WP

I was a RAGPICKER today. I went walking and found a house that had a lot of stuff out front. Sunday is a good day to find things because people clean up on the weekend + get the stuff out for Monday's pick up.

Somebody must have D. I got some old magazines, a

wig, an ashtray with mosaic tile, an old doll with missing arms, + some wood slats. Maybe the Antique Mart will buy the magazines. I will have to stop there tomorrow + ask. I will make something with the rest of the stuff.

I have made 2 THINGS in this house already. One is a big clear plastic bag filled with dried leaves, 2 light bulbs, straps from a watch, + an old wedding announcement. Everything I make is named after the street + number so this one is called 1002 5th Avenue. Then I have a big-brimmed straw sun hat with shiny buttons that I sewed on + old jars of fingernail polish. The top of the hat is missing + inside it I glued Styrofoam peanuts. That's 2421 S. Roosevelt. SHE called me names when SHE saw me sewing. I just kept sewing.

Today's will be 503 S. Robert.

I am looking at OUR picture again. The picture from the closet. In it I am eight years old, standing in front of our WV house on Easter morning. You are wearing a brown dress with red lines crisscrossing it like windowpanes. You have on a pearl necklace + red lipstick. Your hair is auburn + wavy. You look beautiful. I am wearing gray pants + a blue blazer. I have a red clip-on bow tie. We are holding hands. We are smiling.

I should have never let go of your hand. I should have known what was going to happen. I should have

I hate pictures. I HATE this picture. It reminds me of US. It shows me what will never happen again. I HATE it. But I could never hide it in a box on the top shelf of a closet. I could never throw it out for the trash men. It's mine forever. I am keeping it (in my 5403). But I took a clear plastic report cover, cut it to your picture's size, and taped it around you. This way you (+ I) will last forever.

+ THEYLL NEVER KNOW.

Monday, November 28
427 WP

Dear Jenny,

Mrs. Pope handed me a note at the beginning of class. It said: Why didn't you come back on Saturday? You have to be brave. Maybe you can try again.

Afterwards she was waiting for me.

Where's your extra credit?

I said: I don't know what to write.

I thought she might say more about coming back to her house. But she didn't. She gave me a topic + said I should hand it in for Wednesday: Something I Don't Like to Do. I THINK a million things about that, but I have nothing to WRITE or SAY OUT LOUD about it. I will have to find something. I want extra credit.

After school I went to the Antique Mart + asked if they wanted to buy the magazines I found. There were some National Geographics, Lifes, + Times.

We have too many Geographics, the man said. Also, we don't buy Times. But these Lifes look okay. I'll give you 25c each.

I had 5 of them, so I made $1.25. I am going to go out looking for more things tomorrow.

Afterwards I passed a McDonald's on Apache Blvd. There in the front window was a sign: NOW HIRING. JOIN OUR TEAM TODAY. It was like the sign was written for me. I went in. My brain thought I could fill out an application + make money. It was a mistake because as soon as I got to the counter, my nose smelled that good greasy hamburger smell + my mouth wanted 1 (or 2). But I only had 45c, because after I went to the Antique Mart I had stopped at Pic'n'Save + bought 2 candy bars for 80c. It was a special. I should have waited because I had enough money for a regular hamburger before I bought the candy bars.

The McGirl behind the counter handed me an application. When I gave it back to her, she said I would have to see the manager, except he was busy on Drive Through.

What should I do? I asked.

Sit down + wait, she said.

I was sitting in the smoking section because that's where the only empty table was, when I saw another McGirl start wiping tables + cleaning up. I wasn't paying much attention except that I thought she looked familiar. Then she turned + looked right at me, + I could tell it was S.

My feet wanted to leave. She hadn't talked to me since she called. My eyes couldn't look at her (unless she wasn't looking at me) + my mouth couldn't say the dialog with her. How could it say Spanish words with witnesses? When it was our turn to do the dialog in front of the class, my mouth mumbled: don't know. So S did it alone + probably got an A. I got an F.

S said: Well, if it isn't senor albondigas.

S was making fun of me, because the dialog I couldn't do was about meatballs (albondigas).

I said (not very loud): See (except that my brain meant Si).

S said: Buenos dias, senor boca grande.

Now she was really making fun of me, but I was trying not to notice. My nose was smelling hamburgers, my eyes were zeroing in on somebody's partially eaten hamburger sitting unwrapped at the empty table next to mine. Could I eat it? Would I eat it? If no one was watching?

I said: See sen yur

S said: What?

I said: eye doan

no

My brain was thinking English, but my mouth was making weird sounds.

S said: Don't talk to me if you don't want to. I don't want to disturb you.

Yur knot, I said.

Are you waiting for your order? Did you have a grill?

I started to shake my head.

Waiting for someone?

Manager.

You want to see Carlos?

Uh.

Are you trying to get a job here?

My mouth didn't have to say anything, because Carlos showed up then + wanted to know what he could do for me.

S moved away + started wiping a table.

I want, could I have a job? I said.

You want to work after school?

Yes.

Your parents don't mind?

No.

Have you worked anywhere before?

No.

I don't have any openings now, but keep checking.

But I thought

He was gone + his words didn't match what my eyes had seen on the sign in the window. Maybe he didn't like the looks of me.

S started wiping a table near me. She said, I'm only working till 6. If you come back then, I can tell you more about working here. We can walk home together. I live on the street behind you, remember?

My brain thought: LEAVING HOUSE LEAVING HOUSE. Like it was a big red emergency sign flashing. FLASHING. How how HOW???

But I said

OK

I felt OK (not HAPPY). I had a little money in my pocket.

I came home + locked myself in. I want to be good — just in case stepnother is looking for trouble. Now I'm waiting for dinner.

930 RP (radio time)

I watched the clock all the way through dinner: soup beans + hambone + a Jiffy cornbread mix. Afterwards, I asked Roger if I could use his bike for a while. He said OK. At 546 WP I said, I'm going out riding Roger's bike. I want to look for something at Osco. I'll just be gone awhile, I said. It was dark + cool + other parents might have said NO. Child grabbers might be lurking. But THEY didn't care if I was grabbed, only if someone wanted money for me. + THEYd never pay.

I rode like H to McDonald's.

S was waiting at the tables in front.

I didn't think you were coming, she said.

I didn't know what to say. I got off the bike +

started pushing it as we walked across the parking lot.

For a while, S didn't say anything either.

It's not a bad job, she said after we crossed Mill + headed down University. But you won't get rich working there.

Then she said, Do you want to go to my favorite place?

I didn't know.

You have to talk, she said, or I'm going home. I don't need to talk to a zombie, you know.

OK, I said.

OK what? she asked.

Your favorite place.

She led me to Roosevelt School, only it's not Roosevelt School anymore. It's nothing, just a building that D a few years ago I guess. Now it sits there with its doors + windows covered with plywood. There are some swings left, so we sat on them.

S said: I've never told anyone this is my favorite place. I come here a lot when I need to think. What's your favorite place?

My shoulders shrugged.

I wasn't going to tell her about your BR. About your soft bed floating in the night.

You don't like to talk much, do you?

My head shook a no.

S said: I know, sometimes I'm like that. I don't want to talk, or I can't. Like my mouth won't even open. I get like that after I see a really sad movie. Or when my Mom's having a fit. Or when I get some bad news + I get depressed + in a mood, I mean a MOOD, a REAL MOOD + I can't talk. Has that ever happened to you?

My mouth said (I don't go) before I ever knew I was answering her.

Then I had to stop + swallow + say: (To movies).

S said: Well, do you ever feel like English is a foreign language sometimes? Like you can say all the words inside your head perfectly but when they come out of your mouth it's like you've never learned them at all? Like they're sounds you never learned to pronounce?

Then my mouth opened up + words rushed out in bunches:

Like they're alive
in my head
but they aren't
when they come out.
Except

Except what? she asked.

Except now.

Now this minute

they aren't. But

(S was waiting for me to finish)

they could start again.

Start what? she asked.

Start not being alive.

(I couldn't say D, I couldn't say D.)

S: Now why couldn't you talk like that in Spanish?

She was smiling at me. Just like YOU (I thought). Like she had a warm fire inside her + I was freezing. She could make me feel warm, if I let her. But I'm a freezy snowman + her fire would melt me to D.

I looked at Ss face. The streetlight was shining right on it. Ss skin was creamy white + beautiful + I wanted to touch it + feel how soft it was. I wanted to hug S + feel Ss hair on my cheek.

I wanted S to be YOU.

I knew I wanted too much.

She stopped her swing then + looked right at me: I know you watch me at school. I see you looking. Not just in Spanish, but whenever you pass me walking down the hall. At first it scared me. I thought there was something really wrong with you. I guess that's why I called you about the dialog. I could tell you liked me + I thought you'd start being friendly. Only I scared you, I think. You seem kind of lost, but you're not scary. Actually, I think you're kind of interesting if you'd just start talking. I don't know about the other stuff, though.

What stuff?

The garbage stuff.

D

ing

d

ing

d

Why do you go through the garbage cans at school?

I started to count the wrinkles on my knuckles. 123456789

You know that some kids call you The Junkman, don't you?

1011121314151617181920

I'm not trying to embarrass you. I just want to know, that's all. It's something I've wondered about.

My mouth closed, my eyes closed, my brain closed.

Then I disappeared (except for my ears).

I'm not trying to give you a hard time. But I mean do you know how strange it looks to see some cute-looking guy

(my head wasn't moving but my eyes opened + snuck towards her then + she saw)

walking down the hall, talking to himself, then digging through the garbage.

Then she said: + I saw you looking at me just now. So I know you're listening.

My mouth said: You're lying.

S: About what?

M: I don't talk to myself.

S: Yes you do. I've heard you in Spanish. Did anyone ever tell you that you think too much?

My ears listened to the chain on my swing creak + stretch. My brain was thinking: If I opened my mouth + answered her, would it snap + fracture my skull? Or would it keep holding me up so I could talk?

M: No one really talks to me.

S: That's sad.

M: I don't want anyone to talk to me.

S: Do you want me to talk to you?

M: You aren't talking, you're lying.

S: OK, maybe I'm wrong. Maybe you don't talk to yourself, but you go through trash cans. Don't you?

My brain didn't want to tell her anything, but my mouth did it anyway.

M: I look for things.

Nothing snapped. Again.

S: Like what?

(I was listening to my emptiness, my nothingness)

You can tell me.

M: Things.

S: What things?

M: I build things.

S: What kind of things?

M: Just things. From what I find.

S: What do you do with them?

M: Nothing. I hang them up. Then I make more things.

S: Can I see them sometime?

M: I don't know.

S: Are you going to talk to me tomorrow at school?

M: I don't know.

S: Do you want to talk to me again? Like we were friends maybe?

M: I don't have any friends.

S: I know. Maybe that's why I want to talk to you. Don't get me wrong. I don't mean boyfriend. I'm seeing somebody. I just mean regular friends.

I didn't know how to talk about being friends. So my eyes looked at your watch. 607 WP

WRONGTIME WRONGTIME

M: What time?

S looked at her watch.

S: A little after 730.

M: But what time?

S: What?

M: Exactly what time?

738, S said.

I tried to wind your watch but it wouldn't wind. Your watch was out of time.

I've got to go.

I didn't even say goodbye. I just jumped on the bike + rode home.

THEY yelled at me. YOULL NEVER GO ANY-WHERE AGAIN. WE WERE OUT LOOKING FOR YOU. THERES STUFF MISSING AGAIN.

It wasn't a dollar from HER jewelry box?

No: it was more chocolate chips. A box of (stale) Ding Dongs.

SHE always goes to the Hostess Thrift Shop to buy week-old stuff. The older it is, the cheaper it is. SHEll buy 5 or 6 boxes of Ding Dongs + then put them in our lunches for a month. They're so stale you can break your teeth on them.

I didn't take anything, I said.

I CAN SEE I MADE A MISTAKE. I THOUGHT YOU LEARNED YOUR LESSON LAST WEEK WHEN YOU STOLE THOSE CHOCOLATE CHIPS. I ONLY LOCKED YOU IN ONE NIGHT BECAUSE I THOUGHT ID GIVE YOU A BREAK. BUT IVE HAD IT WITH YOUR STEALING. YOUR DOORLL BE LOCKED EVERY NIGHT FROM NOW ON SO YOUD BETTER GET USED TO IT. ROGERS SLEEPING IN THE LIVING ROOM FROM NOW ON. IVE ALREADY TALKED TO YOUR F. WERE GETTING HIM A FOLDOUT COUCH. I DONT WANT HIM SLEEPING WITH A THIEF.

Then the Ding Dong Robber better not sleep with himself, I thought.

So now I'm in my GB. My very own GB. The door's locked. No one will come in. It feels private, like my OWN HOME. I know I should be M, I know I should be screaming, but I can't do it now. Now I'm just glad I have my own BR, even if the door's locked. Even if it is a BIG LIE.

Jennie just knocked at my SR window.

What are you doing here? I asked her.

This is the only way I can talk to you now that the door's locked.

The lock makes it mine. Now it's MY ROOM.

The witch is killing you. You love what you hate.

How could I do that?

Just wait till the chips are missing again. Wait till the Ding Dong tolls for you. They might put bars on the window. You've got to get out before you're locked in.

I can still talk to you through the bars.

Not if they take out the window + put in cinder blocks.

But they wouldn't do that. It'd cost too much money.

It depends on how much their hate is worth.

Then she disappeared.

Am I lying? Was I imagining her?

She was there, I saw her. We talked.

Just like I talked to you.

Just like I am talking to you now.

I know.

Tuesday, November 29
7:32 RP

Dear Jenny,

Your watch is broken and I feel like I'm running on different time, somebody else's time now. Your watch was old, old enough not to use a battery, old enough to be wound. It belonged to your M. It was a little fancy, but HE must have hated it (or you or your M) and so HE threw it out. I will take it to a jewelry store this week and try to get it fixed.

I talked to S in Spanish: Hi (but I couldn't look at her). S said I should go back to McD's today. That's how she got her job, by going back and back and back. So I did and Carlos said: be here tomorrow at 3:30 and the job's yours. Don't be late and be ready to mop floors and clean tables, 20 hours a week, and payday is Friday. Cash. McMoney. What beautiful words.

And S.

Maybe we can walk to Roosevelt School.

Now I am going to write Mrs. Pope's assignment for extra credit:

SOMETHING I DON'T LIKE TO DO

I don't like to talk. Or write. Or communicate to anyone.

I just like to think.

(To myself)

When I talk to or write for someone else, they take my words and turn them into things I never meant. Triangles meant to be squares. Numbers meant to be letters. Long words meant to be abbrev. Hot words meant to be cold. Outside words meant to stay (inside).

Talking isn't as real as thinking. My brain is undisturbed by things outside it. My brain is a safe place. The words I say are air. They disappear and evaporate or become clouds in someone else's eyes. They are not pure.

But I am writing this for someone. I am writing this for a grade. Does that mean I do things I don't want to do, just because they are expected? Because they are demanded? Because I want to fit in and be happy? Because I don't want to be punished? Or have my head removed and served for someone's charbroiled dinner (before a Ding Dong Dessert)?

Can I start a paragraph

in the middle of a sentence? Can I say things in (parentheses)?

Can I indent a paragraph
                                                  as far
                                                                  as I
want?

Do I have to use quotation marks or can people just talk?

{I don't know. What do you think?}

<I think you have a point but don't be surprised by the criticism>

Or do I have to follow the rules, follow the rules, follow the rules, follow the rules, follow the rules rules rules rules rules rules just to make some English teacher happy.

?

Can I RIGHT what I want + still be HAPPY? Or does someone else have to approve?

Why can't thinking cause a person to be happy? Why can't my brain be enough? There are no echoes, no silences inside me. There is me and the running stream of my thoughts. There are no judgments, no sneers inside me.

There is just me

+ the wish for

contentment.

I have written enough.

Now I want to (think).

I start writing and all this stuff gets put together. Writing is like making THINGS. Actually, life is like making THINGS.

Go to bed, Julian.

But I have to rewrite Mrs. Pope's paper.

Then rewrite it and put your brain to bed for the night.

Yes, master.

Thursday, December 1
10:05 RP

Dear Jenny,

My first two McDays were okay. I didn't write about it yesterday because I was tired. I scrubbed a lot of tables and McMopped the floors. I cleaned the bathrooms too. Carlos wanted to show me how to mop, but I already knew how. I think he was impressed.

Did you work someplace else before here? he asked.

No, I said, I just work a lot at home.

Working at McD's is a lot like working at home. Except I don't have to put up with CERTAIN PEOPLE and the food is better. I can watch the cook put a Big Mac on the tray, and I can watch the assistant manager wrap it up, and I can take it. Hot Fresh. Mine. Plus I get paid McMoney. Tomorrow.

Carlos said if I did a good job I could learn how to fry. I guess that's the best job to have. S didn't work yesterday but she worked today. She was working a cash register so I didn't see too much of her. But if I was her customer I would have bought a hot apple pie every time she asked.

I felt funny when I had to change the garbage bags. I pulled out the bag and tied it shut. Then I put a new bag in the can. I know S was watching me. I know there was only food in the bag and cups and containers, but part of me was itching to look through it. Somebody might have thrown away something interesting. But I couldn't do it.

I was probably talking to myself too.

S didn't walk home with me. Some guy in a black Bronco came to get her. The earring in his left ear was sparkling. She said goodbye and that was all.

Something happened with Mrs. Pope today. She asked me to stay after class.

I read your paper, she said. I really liked it. And I hope you're writing something else for me.

Like what?

Anything. I told you I'd give you extra credit.

But I don't know what to write.

Your novel, remember?

I can't do that.

Sure you can, she said. The story of your short but full life.

Uh-uh.

Well, why don't you try writing a short paper with the title The Story of My Life? Then we'll see what happens. You could do that and hand it in next week. You could even try to make an enormous sacrifice and standardize your writing format a little.

I'll try.

Maybe you can stop by this weekend.

I've got a job now, I said. I'm working at McD's.

You must be very busy then.

(Was she making fun of me?)

Work hard on your story, she said.

That was all there was to say.

Friday, December 2
9:17 RP

Dear Jenny,

Carlos didn't want me to start work until 4:30 RP today so I went home first. I was sitting in my GB when I heard the doorbell ring, only I didn't think anything of it because it would never be for me.

WRONG

There was STEPNOTHER q u i e t l y unlocking the door to my room.

There was S standing in the doorway.

There was the P can (full) sitting in the middle of the floor.

"Hi," she said.

(Yes, I will try to use quotation marks even though I hate them. They look PRISSY — a STEPNOTHER word.)

I was trapped, dissolving, fading away.

"You could at least say hi."

You know what I did/didn't say.

"I saw the schedule for today. We're both working at 4:30, so I thought I'd stop by and we could go to work together."

I wasn't talking/moving only thinking:

OUTOFTHEROOM OUTOFTHEROOM

"Are these your THINGS?" she asked, looking at the wall above my bed.

OUTOFTHEROOM

"Yeah."

"I like them," she said.

OUTOFTHEROOM OUTOFTHEROOM

"I like your bed, too."

How could she like my bed? I was twisting my thumb so hard I almost pulled it off.

"Does your roof have a leak?"

She was looking at the P can. My brain was thinking: it just says Maxwell House, not P. Butwhatifshesmellsit? Butwhatifshesmellsit?

Then I saw words inside my head like a billboard. I read them to her. They came out fast: "I can't go with you now."

"What's wrong?"

I had radiation poisoning from her x-ray eyes.

"I've got a headache," I said. "You go without me. I'll be there later."

But I didn't want to go to work. I didn't want to see her. What if she knew about the lock on my door? What if she knew about the P can? What if she knew about the bed? What if she knew I could see her from my SR window?

What if? What if

At McD's she said, "You're having some kind of weird day, right?"

My mouth was empty.

She gave me a hot-apple-pie smile. "I'm having one, too. With you."

We didn't say much after that. We just worked. Then we got paid. I got paid for working eight hours. $26.44. I knew it would make me feel good to make money. It's almost a year's worth of MM, I couldn't believe it.

She walked with me into the parking lot. Together.

My brain figured that her eyes were searching for the Bronco. "I thought I had a date tonight," she said. "But I guess I don't. You want to do something?"

"Can't," I said.

Her eyes searched my face.

"OK," she said. "Then I'll walk you home."

"Why?"

She was scaring me.

"Because I want to," she said. "I hate walking home alone."

"I have to go someplace," I said.

"Where?"

"Jewelry store," I said.

"For what?"

"Get a watch fixed."

"I'll come with you."

How could I stop her?

The jeweler told me it would be cheaper (in the long run) to get a new watch. But I didn't want the long run. I want to live my life on your time.

The man said, "I'll give you a good deal."

"Can, I mean, could you fix it?"

S was watching each word.

"Okay, I'll take a look at it. But it won't be less than 20 or 30 dollars. Why don't you come back next Friday?"

I will look for extra junk. I will spend my McMoney on it.

Outside, S said, "That's really nice. Fixing your XXXXXX's watch.

(fingernails on a blackboard)

What

is it, a surprise for her?"

"No."

We didn't say anything else the rest of the way to my house.

"What's the matter with you tonight?" she asked.

I shrugged.

"If you didn't want company, why didn't you just say so?"

"I don't know."

I walked inside without saying anything else.

Now I feel terrible. And it's all because of S. How can I be her friend when there's a P can in my bedroom? When she thinks that a NOTHER is my M? When the NOTHER has to unlock the door to let her in?

Unlock the door yourself.

I can hear Jennie's voice saying that.

How do I unlock the door?

Be Ss friend.

I'm afraid to be her friend.

You've got to try.
Try.

I don't want to try. I'm sick of trying. Why can't I just be OK?

You wouldn't be you, Junkman, P Can, in McMop Land.

11:05 RP

I did something strange (for me). I looked out my window at Ss house. The light was on in her window, and I thought I could see her shadow. Without thinking really, I opened my window and jumped outside. I didn't even stop to wonder what would happen if THEY found out. Probably because my door was locked and there was no reason to come into my room. But THEY were still up, so I walked quietly to the back gate and opened it, crossed the alley, and found Ss gate. I didn't even wonder if she had a dog, I just opened the gate and went to her window and tapped.

When she didn't come to the window, I realized how stupid I was. What if she was calling the cops? What if she had a gun?

Why were my feet even doing this? What did my mouth want to say?

All whispery, it said, "Susan."

It was the first time my mouth ever said her name in the air.

"Susan."

Then my hand tapped again.

"Susan."

My eyes saw a shadow, then her face. S opened the curtains and slid the window back.

"What are you doing?" she asked. "Why are you here?"

My brain thought about running. But my mouth opened and said, "2 talk. 2 U."

It was that foreign language, but she could understand me.

"Just a second." She went to her door and locked it. Then she grabbed a sweater and opened the screen on the window. "Out of the way, Julian. I'm coming out."

We sat with our backs leaning on the house.

"I'm kind of surprised," she said. "Especially after you wouldn't talk to me tonight. I mean, I take it you're here to tell me something."

What could my mouth say in words that she'd understand?

Jennie was trying to help.

WHAT DO YOU WANT TO SAY?

TALK ABOUT THE THINGS THAT MATTER.

"My mouth doesn't know how to say anything," I said.

"Then just try saying one thing," she said.

Some words started to float toward the air.

"You saw my room."

"I know," S said. "I wanted to talk about that, but we didn't get very far tonight."

"Did you see things there?"

"Yes, I saw the THINGS you made."

"No, not my THINGS. Other things. Did you see strange things?"

"I saw you and your THINGS and your room."

"And the — "

My mouth stopped.

"And the what?"

"Nothing," I said. "I don't know."

"I don't know either," S said.

TRY SOMETHING ELSE.

"The watch," I said.

"What about it?"

"It's not for

(no word, no word)

It belongs to my M, but not the one at home."

"Your M? What do you mean your M?"

"You know," I said, "everybody has one."

"You mean your — "

My mouth wouldn't let her finish. "Yes. My M."

"So it's not your M's watch?"

"Yes," I tried to explain again, "but not the one at home."

"You mean you have two Ms?"

"No, well, yes, kind of."

"You mean the one now is your step-M or something like that?"

My head said yes. "And it's not HER watch."

"Okay, it's not her watch. So it's your M's watch. Your real M."

"Yes," I said. Our words were floating on the surface. "And it's my watch now. I wear it around my neck."

"Julian, I don't understand. Is this a riddle or something?"

"Maybe. I don't know."

"What do you want to tell me?"

I breathed for a long time until I could say four more words.

"I
saw
a
movie."

"I thought you didn't go to movies." Then she said: "What movie?"

"I
   it's
      called"

"What?"

"It's
      an
         old
             movie."

The words started to connect
                        "About something
                                                something strange."

"What about it?"

"I like it
              I want it
                            to be
                                 real."

"What's it about?"

"I don't know
                   how to tell you."

"Where'd you see it?"

"On TV."

"Well, maybe it's on video. Maybe we could rent it and watch it one night."

WE WE WE all the way home.

"Can you tell me what it's called?"

Shaking no.

"Do you know the title?"

Nodding.

"But you can't say it?"

Yes.

"You CAN'T say it?" she repeated.

Then my mouth whispered something she barely heard: (out loud)

"Then why are you telling me about this?"

"I want you to know."

"Well, can you write it? I see you writing like crazy in Spanish sometimes."

My H was leaving my body.

"Here," S said. "I'll go inside and get some paper. Okay? And, remember, I know where you live."

She was gone and I breathed 36 times till she wasn't gone anymore.

Then there was an nb in my hands and a pen between my fingers. It felt like the first pen ever invented. It was something new, strange. My brain knew the words to write, but my fingers couldn't move the pen. Everything began to feel fuzzy and dim and the words in my head were starting to melt away.

Without thinking, my hand wrote: 90J

"90J?"

My hand crossed it out, then wrote:

P O R

T R A

I T O F J

"Por?" she asked. "It's Spanish?"

The picture in my brain disappeared.

"Just a minute, what is this?" she asked studying the letters. "Portrait. Oh, I see. Portrait of J. Is that it?"

My head nodded.

"I know: Portrait of Julian Drew."

"That would be a black

I mean, blank picture."

"Maybe on top, but underneath there's a whole world nobody can see. You're an iceberg, Julian — "

"I'm not that big," I said. "I'm a snowman, a drowning snowman."

She gave me the paper again. "Don't change the subject. Portrait of who?"

My mouth opened and one word flew out.

"Jennie."

The word was alive.

"The girl's name?" she asked.

"Yes. But IE not Y."

"Portrait of Jennie," S said. "90J."

My body was shaking now.

"Maybe I can rent it at a video store. That's what you want, isn't it? For me to see the movie and understand?"

"Yes."

"You're shivering."

I nodded.

"What is it about your room and the watch and this movie? I don't understand any of this. But I'll tell you something. You're doing a great job of taking my mind off my problems."

Her problems. I wasn't even thinking about her problems. I was thinking about me and how I was feeling: very strange, but not like I wanted to RA. It reminded me of the last night I spent with YOU. HE was at work. We were lying side by side and YOU were C and I was C. It was the middle of the night. Then YOU were sick in the washtub and afterwards YOU got groggy and asked me to put that cold washcloth on your forehead. So I did while YOU fell asleep. Then I fell asleep and when I woke up YOU were gone.

I wondered what S would think if she knew all

about me. I wondered how I could ever be okay: to talk like I write, to be like I think. But I didn't say anything to her. I just counted my breaths. Fifteen. Sixteen.

"I should go," I said.

"I'm glad you came over," S said. "I'll see you at work tomorrow."

Then she leaned over and kissed my cheek.

And stood up.

And went inside.

I can still feel where she kissed my cheek. The skin feels different there. It didn't feel like your kisses.

It felt like S.

Saturday, December 3
10:43 RP

S surprised me tonight, kind of ambushed me. She was done at 6:00 RP but I had to work through dinner rush till 8:00 RP. She said goodbye, and I kept working. But when I punched out at 8:03 RP, S was waiting for me.

"Look what I have," she said.

She showed me: VIDEO 90J

No breath at all.

"I had to look for it at a bunch of stores, but I found it. You want to watch it tonight? My M's spending the weekend at her boyfriend's. Can you come over?"

Three breaths.

"Call your parents

(I DONT HAVE PARENTS)

and

tell them you have to work till 11:00."

One breath. "I can't. They'll know."

"Then I'll call them. I'll tell them that I'm the assistant manager."

I stopped breathing. "You can't."

"Yes, I can. Darlene does it all the time for me when I want to go somewhere."

With the sparkling earring, my brain thought. And where is somewhere?

She was standing by the pay phone. She put a quarter in and started punching my number.

"But what if they know?"

"They're not going to kill you," she said. "They're just parents. And they won't find out."

Then she did it.

"Hello? Mrs. Drew? This is Darlene. I'm the assistant manager at the Apache Boulevard McDonald's, where Julian works? I just wanted to call and let you know that I need him to work until 11:00 tonight . . . Someone called in sick . . . Yes, you know, he's one of our best workers. He may even become Employee of the Month soon. Thank you, Mrs. Drew." She hung up the phone. "See how easy that was?"

The world didn't end.

But it was shaking.

S took me home and we watched the movie. It was like I found a billion dollars on the street (MM forever) but I was afraid somebody was going to come and take it away from me. What if a plane crashed on the house? What if a gas line exploded? What if Ss mother came home and found us?

What if I D?

S sat on the couch, my body took the chair. My brain couldn't think about sitting near her. My eyes were looking at shining gold the whole time. I memorized everything. I repeated what I could (inside). My brain was working triple overtime.

Eben Adams was the painter, Jennie Appleton was the girl. She played a wishing game with him. He saw her seven times:

in the park
at the ice rink
the night her parents D
the time he painted her picture
at the convent
at the park when she graduated from college
and
OCTOBER 5TH.

October 5th was the day she D. That was the day he found her. That was the day they were together.

HE TRAVELED BACK THROUGH TIME TO GET TO HER.

And the weirdest thing of all: OCTOBER 5TH was the day that I began dreaming about YOU. My dream about a letter in a book in an old bookcase started 10/5. Not her year, but my year. THIS YEAR. Maybe I knew about this. Why did they both happen on the same day?

Does this mean something?

Jennie sings a song (my song, OUR song) in the movie. I know the book-song by H, but the movie-song is longer. After the Wind Blows and the Sea Flows and Nobody Knows, Jennie sings: "And where I am going, nobody knows." My brain thinks she was singing to me. Now I know ALL the words, and I will NEVER forget the tune.

Watching the movie was like seeing a ghost. Of YOU. It was like watching US. Or maybe it was like seeing the future. How I could see YOU again.

The whole time, I was keeping my foot on YOU in my shoe. I was rubbing my foot to keep in touch. I was pressing so hard, like I was giving CPR.

Only I wasn't.

When the movie was over I couldn't talk.

But S did.

"Is something wrong with your shoe?"

"No," I said.

S said, "I liked that movie."

"Me too."

"Why is it so important?"

how to say, what to say, not to say: show SHOW!

I took YOU out of my shoe.

"90J," I said.

"90J," S said.

"My 90J. Do you understand?"

Breathing.

"Who is 90J?" S asked.

"My M."

"Which M?"

"My real

(I pointed to where I wore your watch)

not

the replacement."

"Where is she?"

Breathing, breathing.

"Wheeling. West Virginia. Where I used to live."

"When was the last time you saw her?"

"Four years, six months, and two days ago."

You were in Greenwood.

"Do you ever talk to her?" My brain was turning spongy.

"I write her. Almost every day."

"But she never calls you?"

"She can't."

"But why not? Won't your — " and she started to say an XXXXXX word.

"F," I told her. "He's my F."

She didn't laugh. She didn't look confused. She just said, "Won't your F let you talk to your M?"

"They won't let me do anything."

"They let you be here tonight."

"That's because they don't know."

"They let you work."

"They keep me

(my brain was thinking, my mouth was ready)

under lock and key."

She didn't understand.

"I remember your favorite place," I said. "It's Roosevelt School. Now I'll tell you mine. It's Wheeling."

"Can't you go there? To see your M?"

"Maybe."

"When?"

"Don't know."

"Can't she send you the money to visit her?"

"No, that's why I'm working."

"You must XXXX your M a lot."

"No. I L my M."

"You L your M?"

I nodded.

"Well, I don't L mine at all."

"You don't?"

"Not the way she treats me. Have you ever — ?"

Before she could say anymore, the phone rang. S said 23 words:

"Where were you last night?/Yeah right/You could've/No I can't/Because/Well but not/All right but you better show up."

Then she hung up with fuzzy eyes.

"I've got to get ready to go out," she said.

I didn't stick around to answer her question. I put YOU away and went home. No one yelled at me. Maybe I smelled too much like hamburgers.

And now I am singing our 90J song.

Sunday, December 4
1:17 RP

Almost all I could think (and sing) about today was 90J. Then my brain got a crazy idea. I went to ASU library and typed TIME TRAVEL in the computer catalog. I thought the computer would say NO ENTRIES ON THIS SUBJECT but I was wrong. The computer wrote PRACTICAL TIME TRAVEL on the screen. There was a book number. QB209. I almost couldn't write it down. My right arm and hand turned into concrete. I went to the QB section, worried that the book would be gone. But there it was: faded pink sitting on the shelf. When I touched it, I felt electricity like I was being shocked. Then I sat down at a desk and my eyes started to look at it. No one had checked it out for 15 years. It had been waiting FOR ME for 15 years. And each word was perfect, like I had read it all before.

Traveling through time. The book says if you're going to go back in time, you need to be in the place you want to travel to. You can only travel back or forth in time, not to different places. I wondered how I could get to WV to go back to YOU.

I wanted to be a thief (the kind Stepnother thinks I am) and keep the book. I wanted to take it with me. But there are alarms in the library and I didn't want to get caught. I thought about hiding the book behind other books so nobody else could ever check it out, but somebody might find it and move it somewhere else. Instead I am memorizing how to travel to YOU:

1. Go to the place you want to be when you travel.
2. Surround yourself with THINGS from the time you want to travel to.
3. Isolate yourself from the outside world.
4. Wait for it to happen.
5. Snowy or rainy days are best because bad weather seems to make time travel more possible.

GO TO THE PLACE, SURROUND, ISOLATE, WAIT, AND BAD WEATHER.

I tried to write Mrs. Pope's assignment today, but it didn't work. I was too busy thinking about 90J and singing that song and memorizing how to find you. I can hear the words in my head right now.

This is what I wrote. It is not good.

THE STORY OF MY LIFE

> Here are the facts:
>
> I was born in Wheeling, West Virginia.
> My mother died on June first a few days after I finished fifth grade. My father remarried three months later. My stepmother had two children of her own. Then my father and my stepmother had another child. They did not treat me well. We moved to Arizona. They did not treat me well there either.

I hate facts.

Why does it sound so stupid when I put the facts down? Facts don't help people understand. My life isn't facts. It's the way my STEPNOTHER smiles this slickly sick smile when SHE hands me a soggy pancake. It's the way HE puffs on his crackling pipe when

HEs ignoring me. It's the way Roger pretends to sneeze and says "Horse S" so he can cover up one of his smelly Fs. It's the way I feel about Emma being YOUR baby BUT living with HER.

I will try again tomorrow.

In the meantime I am going to think of how to find YOU. I am going to find a way to travel.

TO YOU.

One of these days

One of these ways

Monday, December 5
(TWO MONTHS after my nowhere dream began)
8:19 RP

I tried Mrs. Pope's assignment again tonight.

THE STORY OF MY LIFE

My life was normal, then it wasn't.
My life was happy, then it wasn't.

My life WAS, then it WASN'T.

I had a M, then I didn't. I had a F, then I didn't.

I didn't have a STEPNOTHER, then I DID.

There was something, then there was nothing. There was a room and a lock with no key.

There was a CAN, then there was a CAN'T.

I am nothing, trying to
                                trying
                                     trying to be

This is no good.

I have been thinking of Jennie. And S. She wasn't at school (or work) today. What will happen if I say I missed her?

I missed her.

Where was she?

Tuesday, December 6
9:52 RP

THEY were out front talking to a neighbor this afternoon. Emma was in her BR. I was playing dolls with her.

"This is the M and this is the little girl," Emma said.

I picked up a wedding-dress Barbie and said, "This is another M. She's the little girl's real M, only the little girl doesn't know it."

"I'm your real M," I said, pretending I was the wedding-dress Barbie.

"She can't have two Ms," Emma said.

"Yes, she can," I said. "When you play dolls you can do anything. And some people have two Ms."

"No, they don't."

"What if the first M went away and then the F married a second M?"

"She's going to be Sleeping Beauty."

"Did you know," I said, "that you have another M? A real one, a nice one?"

"My M is nice."

"You had another M, when we lived in West Virginia."

"No I didn't."

"She's in Heaven now," I said. "That's why you have this M. But she's not your real M. She's your STEP-NOTHER."

"That's not right. I know. You're making up a fib, you fibber."

"I have a picture," I said. I pulled it out of my shoe and showed her. "This is our real M and this is me."

"No it's not," she said. "You're teasing me. Now let's play Sleeping Beauty."

She wouldn't even look at YOU.

S wasn't at school again — or at work. She called in sick.

Is something happening?

THE STORY OF MY LIFE

There is no story of my life. Just a beginning and no middle, no end. The beginning keeps beginning. It goes on and on, never reaching a middle.

I want another beginning. I want to try (or be tried) again. A beginning can be a breath. A blink. A step (sometimes backwards).

It just takes TIME.

It's not enough.

Wednesday, December 7
9:24 RP

S came back today but she didn't say much to me. She said she was sick. But she looked weird. Wild thoughts were flying through her head. They were stopping her from talking to me.

Something did happen. I know it.

Now she knows how weird I am.

Mrs. Pope just called. I didn't need my three minutes.

"Can you baby-sit tomorrow night when I go shopping for Christmas presents?"

I think this is strange. What do I know about baby-sitting? She said she would pay me.

I need extra money.

I said I would.

"How's your extra credit?" she asked.

"Oh, well, I'm having trouble writing it. I don't know what to write."

"Here's what Hemingway always did: He started with the truest sentence he knew. Why don't you try that? Think of the truest sentence you know and write it. Then the rest will follow."

That was all.

THE STORY OF MY LIFE

I am an abused child (but I can't tell you that).

Thursday, December 8
4:12 RP

I don't care what day or time it is. I have been good for a week. I have cleaned the toilets (THEIRS and OURS) and bathroom sinks (every day), emptied the garbage (every day), done the dishes (twice), vacuumed the hall (twice), and made my bed (every day). HE came into my room today and said:

"When do you get paid?"

"What? Why?" That's all I said.

What? Why? That's all I knew how to say.

"I said WHEN?"

"Next week."

"I want half the money for room and board."

"But no one else has to pay money."

"No one else is working."

"It's not fair."

"Who said anything's fair?"

"But I wanted (I was lying, I was going to lie) to buy some Christmas presents. Can't you wait till after Christmas? I won't be able to buy any presents. Please?"

Made me beg. Makes me beg for everything.

"I'll see," HE said.

SHE told him to get the money, I could tell.

"Please?"

Wheels were turning.

"Okay," HE said. "So don't ever say I never gave you a second chance."

I
 won't
      say
         any
            thing.

I need all the money for your watch. It will be ready tomorrow and I will be on your time once again.

8:30 RP

I am at Mrs. Pope's house. Baby-sitting. When I got here, she asked me, "Was that your M on the phone when I called last night?"

I breathed and looked at her.

"She sounded kind of angry. Do you get a lot of phone calls? I know Ms sometimes get annoyed when their teenagers spend too much time on the phone."

Fishing fishing.

"No."

"Oh, I just thought maybe your M had something to do with your attitude. You've really pulled away this week. I don't know what's wrong."

S, me, J, you. Now, and then. Tomorrow.

"Did you start writing that journal? Are you writing that novel? Can you get your thoughts out on paper?"

That is what I am doing, Mrs. P. But inky thoughts don't help.

"Doesn't help."

"Oh, Julian, honey, yes it does. I know. You see, my husband divorced me right before Dylan was born and I started writing when I found out that we were getting a divorce. I started writing an article for the newspaper. Something I just had to say. And it cleared my mind up."

I could hear her kids screaming in the bedroom, playing wild games.

"I can see the look on your face, Julian. I know you'd rather make me disappear than listen to me now, but just try. I know what pain is. I had a terrible childhood. And the last few years haven't been so great either. Sometimes no matter what you do it seems like natural forces are working against you."

My eyeballs started swimming but my lips were stitched closed. It was like aliens were in control of me.

"I know what it looks like when you could C at any moment."

She put her arms around me and hugged. I felt her softness, I smelled her smell. It wasn't the same as you. She was C too."It's OK to C. It's OK," she said.

I didn't want to C anymore with her. I wasn't thinking about her anyway. I was thinking about YOU. Leaving YOU. Grieving YOU. I wanted to feel better but I couldn't. I kept hearing those kids carrying on.

Lucy, the four-year-old, came running in. Mrs. Pope jumped back like I was a hot stove.

"Are you our new baby-sitter? Will you sword fight with me? I won't stab you in the penis."

"Lucy! Don't talk that way!"

But Lucy ran off.

"I think she's still mad about her new baby brother, except he's not so new anymore."

She told me how to take care of the kids and then she left.

There are four kids. Rita is the oldest. She's six. She wouldn't go to bed when I told her and sat up with a pair of scissors cutting up magazines. That's what I thought until I looked closer and saw her using them on a paperback Peter Rabbit book.

Lucy is next. She says wild things. Do you want to see my vagina? Tinkle, bm, tinkle, bm.

Donovan is almost three. He has a runny nose and lots of bruises. He wears a diaper and drinks a bottle. Lucy likes to take his bottle and drink it.

Dylan is almost a year. He sleeps a lot and giggles if you blow air on him and sound like the wind.

Rita put Dylan in the walker and pushed him around. Lucy tried to help. Donovan ran after them. I tried to stop them. Rita said that her M let her do whatever she wanted. She could take Dylan for a ride in the stroller too.

I hid the stroller in the closet.

10:35 RP

I looked out my GB window when I got home. Ss light was off. She isn't there anymore.

Mrs. Pope said to me when she got home, "I hope you can confide in me sometime. I was thinking about you tonight. I hope you can be all right. Be happy, I mean. I hope you can write about everything. I think it will help."

Why can't S talk to me?

How can I help?

Friday, December 9
10:11 WP (Your Time Again)

The man fixed your watch for $33.24.

"It's okay now?"

"I cleaned it," he said. "But it could stop running tomorrow."

"But it's working now?"

"That's what I said."

He held the watch out to show me. Your time was working again.

"33.24," he repeated.

I counted out my McMoney and handed it to him. I still have $19.86 left.

Saturday, December 10
11:04 WP

Your time doesn't make me happy enough right now. S won't talk to me at all. When I see her at school or McD's, her eyes look down. She thinks I'm SICK SICK SICK now (I know it), now that she knows about the movie. I shouldn't have told her. I should never tell anyone anything.

My brain is saying: WhataboutMrsPope?

I say back, Idontknow. I don't know.

What would happen if I changed everything about my life? Maybe I could dye my hair another color and get it cut. Maybe I could wear some different color shirts or socks (not from Kmart). Maybe I could go to school and not look through garbage cans. Maybe I could be friendly and smile and become popular with everyone who mattered. Or maybe I could become SE Hinton or JD Salinger.

Maybe I could become J Drew.

And maybe

yes maybe

one day

maybe

I could find you again.

Sunday, December 11
8:15 WP

This afternoon SHE was making roast beef. SHE got one for PRACTICALLY NOTHING. That's why all of us could eat it. When SHE got it in the oven, SHE said, "EVERYBODY OUTSIDE. WERE GOING TO RAKE THE GRAVEL."

We have a gravel front yard. Blue gravel. You have to rake it and pull the weeds to make it look good. HE was out of town. This is the kind of chore SHE loves to make us (ME) do.

"I have homework," I said.

"YOULL HAVE TO DO IT LATER."

"But I need to do it this afternoon."

"I SAID EVERYBODY OUTSIDE."

I went outside. It was warm and sunny and pulling weeds made me hot and HUNGRY.

"I have to go to the bathroom," I said.

(eyes all over me)

"COME RIGHT BACK."

I thought: HE was out of town. SHE was watching everyone outside. I didn't have to go to the bathroom that much.

So I went into the kitchen and opened the Forbidden

Cupboard. I have never done this before. I took one (small) handful of chocolate chips. They were melting in my mouth when Emma saw me. She had followed me.

"You're not supposed to do that," she said.

"Hmm?"

I couldn't talk yet. I tried to act dumb.

"I'm telling Mommy."

"Emma, don't"

But I couldn't stop her.

"Get in your room" was all SHE said. "GET IN THERE RIGHT NOW! I MEAN IT! DO WHAT YOURE TOLD! AND I MEAN THE FIRST TIME. CHIP SNITCHER!"

The lock was turned.

I did my homework all afternoon.

But I could smell the roast beef and it made me HUNGRY.

At 5:03 WP, I heard someone walk by my door. I thought it was HER.

"Is it dinner time yet?" I called THROUGH THE DOOR.

"YOULL GET YOUR DINNER WHEN ITS READY."

"How long does roast beef take?"

But SHE wouldn't tell me.

At 6:01 WP I was getting worried. SHE wasn't going to give me any dinner. Or SHE was going to make me eat by myself. I knocked on the door.

"Is it time for dinner?

(waiting)

I'm hungry

(waiting)

Is it dinner?"

Nobody would answer.

Feeling like someone took a chainsaw and cut me into pieces and stepped all over me and squashed me into the dirt and bugs ate me until I WAS NOTHING

and Emma helped with the chainsaw.

At 7:08 WP SHE said, "YOUR DINNERS READY."

Click!

SHE escorted me to the table like a prison guard.

Everyone else had eaten, but the house smelled like roast beef. I knew mine would be cold and hard and small and maybe even burnt. But I didn't care as long as it was food.

The table had a spoon and a napkin and a little glass of water.

"Where's my plate?" I asked.

"IM GETTING IT RIGHT NOW," SHE said.

"I need a fork," I said.

"NO YOU DONT," SHE said.

SHE reappeared with a plate full of chocolate chips.

"THIS IS WHAT CHIP SNITCHERS GET FOR DINNER."

The chainsaw was carving up every little leftover piece of me. And 3Rs and Emma were watching. I saw them peering around the corner of the living room. They were smiling and laughing, like I was a TV show.

"I don't want this," I said before she carved up my mouth.

"THEN YOU WONT BE EATING ANYTHING FOR A LONG TIME."

SHE waited a minute.

I wasn't moving.

"IF YOURE NOT EATING IT GET BACK TO YOUR ROOM. MAYBE YOULL WANT IT FOR BREAKFAST."

HE wasn't going to be home until Thursday, but I wasn't going to let HER starve me.

I told HER I was going to bed. I stuffed some clothes in my sleeping bag to make it look like it was full of me, grabbed my McMoney and my jacket, turned off the lights, and opened the SR window. It was raining by then but I didn't care. I was going to Safeway to buy dinner and breakfast and lunch and whatever I needed to not starve.

I didn't care if I got soaked.

Bread, peanut butter, and raspberry jam. I already had plastic knives under my bed. I made four sandwiches and ate them like a chainsawed pig trying to put all the pieces back together.

Tuesday, December 12
10:05 WP

No breakfast and no lunch yesterday (just my PBJ sandwiches) and dinner was ham and beans (only I didn't get any ham with my beans). I couldn't write. My hand wouldn't help me. And there was nothing new to say.

This morning I got food for breakfast and a brown bag for lunch (I ate it on the way to school) and McDinner at work.

I saw Emma this morning at breakfast. She acted like nothing happened, like I never got in trouble. She's only five years old, I know. I know she's not to blame.

But now I don't care. Maybe she's better here. Maybe she doesn't need to know about you.

Maybe I can

GO

SURROUND

ISOLATE

WAIT

and

PRAY FOR BAD WEATHER!

Wednesday, December 13
4:50 WP

Carlos told me I was working after school today so I went in. But the schedule got changed so they sent me home and said to come back at 6:00 WP.

That's when I saw the man. He was in our back yard talking to HER. He was looking at my SR window. Pointing at it.

I opened the window.

"What's wrong?"

"WHY ARENT YOU AT WORK?" SHE asked.

"The schedule got changed. I go in later."

"You'd have the grate come out this far," the man said. He was pointing six inches to the left of my SR window.

"What grate?" I asked.

"SHUT THE WINDOW AND DO YOUR HOMEWORK."

I shut the window but I listened.

"This would keep anybody out," the man said. "I'll send you an estimate. You're sure you don't want to do any other windows?"

"WERE STARTING WITH THIS ONE."

When he was gone, I went into the kitchen. SHE was boiling hot dogs.

"Why are you doing this?" I asked.

The water was bubbling around the top wiener.

"I SAW THOSE MUDDY FOOTPRINTS UNDER YOUR WINDOW," SHE said. "I KNOW YOU SNEAK OUT AT NIGHT. YOU DONT EVEN HAVE TO LIE TO ME. NEXT YOULL BE ROBBING 7–11S. BUT IM GOING TO MAKE SURE YOU DONT."

Now I have to go eat a rubber hot dog and go to McD's. Maybe I won't eat. Maybe I'll just go to work and eat there. Maybe I'll hang out for half an hour.

Maybe I'll make plans to do something else.

Maybe there's nothing more to write about.

Saturday, December 17
11:30 WP

I didn't think I would write in my NB again. Until tonight.

When S knocked at my window.

I was scared. What if THEY saw her? I let her come into my SR and sit down on the floor. They were still up. They could unlock the door. They could come in for an unannounced inspection.

"I've been terrible," she said. "I know. I treated you worse than dirt. I treated you like S. And I know you don't understand. I know I shouldn't be this way, but I can't help it."

My ears were waiting.

"But I want you to understand just the way you wanted me to understand about the movie."

Now my ears were worried.

"I know you don't know anything about me. You probably think I'm this normal person. But I'm really not. When I was in eighth grade, my parents were getting divorced and things were really terrible. Yelling, screaming all the time. I felt like I was XXXXX."

"D," I said.

"OK, I was D inside. Then my — " She paused a moment and looked right at me. "F disappeared and all I had was my M."

Now S was C. Two wet drops rolled down her cheeks.

"I started to think my F hated me or else he would've called me or something. But he was gone. Just took off. I couldn't talk about it. I still can't. My M and I sure never talk about it. I was kind of like you, I guess. I walked around like a zombie or I was a Kleenex freak. And, God, then this year I thought everything was better, but I started — I thought I was being so cool, and I was so dumb. And now I'm paying for it."

Words into questions, but waiting.

She sniffed and wiped her eyes. "I know you like me. You like me too much. You think I'm some kind of great person. But I'm not and I guess I just got tired of treating you like some kind of fragile treasure. I'm just as messed up as you are. I've really F'd up everything. I feel like I'm going crazy. I mean I'm just rattling on and I know I'm probably too much for you to handle. I can't even handle me. But I know you understand. I know. You don't even have to say anything."

Understand. There was no information to understand.

"Start with one thing," I said.

She smiled at me.

"I — "

Sounds moving in the hallway. A rat pack waiting.

She left

but first

there was one more cheek kiss.

A lip-pressed cheek was all S left.

And NO ONE found out.

Sunday, December 18
9:05 WP

I have a story to tell.

We live on a street that has houses along one side and an irrigation canal on the other. Mostly the canal is covered. You can only tell it's there because of the square concrete control stations every so often. But the canal isn't covered at the far end of the street. You go past a Dead End sign and travel down an old dirt farm road. No houses, only old cotton fields on either side. The road runs alongside the canal there, and the canal isn't covered over.

I walk along that road to school sometimes.

That's where I watched S walk on her way to school.

I walked along in back of her.

Watching every step.

Watching every puff of dust that her shoes kicked up.

Only now there wouldn't be any dust because it has been raining here. You can see the tiny craters where raindrops have landed in the dust layer that coats the irrigation canal road.

The road was a place I felt good. It was like being somewhere (nowhere?) else.

Now my story changes. I woke up this morning and heard noise in the kitchen. I got dressed and waited for the door to be unlocked. Then I went into the living room and smelled Roger's P couch that was still open.

"I'm going for a walk," I said.

"YOUR CEREALS HERE."

I just opened the door and left.

I walked down the street until I got to Mrs. Pope's house. Three of her kids were in the driveway, playing. Rita and Lucy were pushing Donovan in his stroller like it was a hot rod. I don't know where Dylan was.

Mrs. Pope was surprised.

"I didn't think I'd see you until Monday," she said.

She was wearing her robe and I looked at her softness. I wondered what it would be like to lie in bed with her in the bedroom of the darkest nights. I wondered how she breathes. I wondered how she floats into dreams.

"You must have something on your mind," she said. "Can I get you something to drink?"

"No," I said.

"Then come into the kitchen and sit down and talk to me."

I sat at the kitchen table. It was brown Formica with a wood grain pattern. A stack of thin white paper napkins sat in the middle. Four plastic cups had four different amounts of orange juice. The table was covered with a crust of dried food and doughnut sprinkles and crumbs and juice spills.

"What's on your mind?" she asked.

"Someone has a problem," I said.

"Someone you know?"

I nodded.

"What kind of problem?"

And before my brain could stop my mouth, it told — NO, I told her about me and them and the lock and P can and burnt hamburgers and plates of chips and Emma and you. And I showed you to her. She looked at you and she listened and winced and understood, oh yes she understood oh so well. She would be able to see, to know. Talking would show her, and then there would be improvement. Advice would be coming. Help was just over the next hill. You were lying on the kitchen table next to the sprinkles.

And she said, "Julian, oh Julian, I knew something was making you so sad. But you have to find a way to get on with your life, you can't be like this forever. That's why you need to write, so you can turn your pain into something beautiful. You can — you know, the whole time you were telling me your story I was thinking of e. e. cummings. Do you know him? Have you read him? You'll read him next year in junior English, but there's one poem that makes me think of you and what you could do with writing."

And she started to read some words from her brain: "If there are any heavens my mother will (all by herself) have one. It will not be a pansy heaven nor a fragile heaven of lilies-of-the-valley but it will be a heaven of blackred roses. My father — "

Then the words stopped.

MOMMYMOMMYMOMMYMOMMYMOMMY

Lucy came running in.

"Donovan fell out of the stroller!"

Heard a thousand times. No panic.

"Well, is he hurt?" Mrs. Pope asked.

"I don't know. We can't find him."

Heard a hundred times. Slight worry.

"Where is he?"

"I don't know. He fell in the water."

Heard once and never again.

"What water?"

Confused

"Where is the water?"

"Across the street."

"OHMYGOD CALL 911 JULIAN!"

She grabbed Lucy and ran away and I made the call.

"A boy fell into the water. We need help," I said. "We really need help. I think he's drowning."

"Where?"

I gave the address, finished explaining, and (I didn't know what else to do) went home.

I didn't know what else to do.

All afternoon a fire truck was parked outside. There's an irrigation control station opposite our living room window. And I saw a fireman in a wet suit climb the ladder down into the irrigation pipe.

Mrs. Pope wasn't there. Neither was Donovan.

And neither were you.

I remembered where you were: on her kitchen table next to the sprinkles.

I thought about how to get you back more than Donovan. Mrs. Pope needed Donovan, but I needed you. More. Much more.

It became night and the red light was still flashing.

I felt sick. I didn't have you.

I could hear the 2-way radio crackle.

Then two firemen climbed back up the ladder. There were four or five men waiting for them. They helped them with something wrapped in a small garbage bag. A woman and a man from an ambulance took the bag and drove away.

Some people walked toward Mrs. Pope's house.

Now everyone is gone.

Except me.

Except

ME.

STEPNOTHER said (peeking out the window): THAT WOMAN DIDNT DESERVE CHILDREN.

Not everyone does, you know.

AND DONT FORGET, THEY ARE COMING TO DO THE GRATE TOMORROW SO MOVE YOUR BOXES OR THEYLL GET DUSTY.

I needed you. So I locked myself in and opened the SR window and climbed out. I knew just where you were on the table. I wasn't going to ring the doorbell. I was going to look in the kitchen window and open the sliding door. But when I got to her window, the table was empty. No cups, no sprinkles, no you.

Then Mrs. Pope was standing by the counter. She was looking right at me. I didn't want to see her. I don't know why. My shoulds were fighting. What should I say, how should I say it?

She opened the sliding door.

She had another face now.

"I can't talk to you."

"I want — "

"What?"

"My picture."

"I don't have it."

"But it was on the — "

"Go away and leave me alone." Her hand was a cleaver cutting air. "I don't have your picture. I don't have it. Why did you come back here?"

This is the end of my story. It is over. And this NB is over. Donovan is over. Mrs. Pope is over. S is over. I don't want to write this but: E is over.

EM

EMM

EMMA

And maybe I am over.

Over and out.

OUT

NB #3:

The

90J(D)

NB

CHAPTER ONE
THE ANSWERS (NOBODY KNOWS)

December 20: a normal day. Bars on window. Lock on door. Blue skies, no rain. Unzipped the sleeping bag like usual and aired it out. Opened the storage room door and selected clothes from Lemon Brillo box.

December 20: turning weird. Pulled on three pairs of underwear and only pair of jeans. Put on three undershirts, one long sleeve shirt, and only sweater. Tried to wear two pairs of socks, but shoes wouldn't fit. So put an extra pair in each jacket pocket. Grabbed jacket and headed for kitchen.

Who did this?

WHO did this?

I did this

I

Picture this: Dressed in many layers of clothes, I walked into a Tempe kitchen on December 20th and saw a bowl of corn flakes and a glass of water sitting on the table waiting patiently for me.

What is wrong with this picture?

[Things To Think About: Who poured the milk on the corn flakes? What purpose was served in pouring it? What condition were the corn flakes in as I entered the kitchen? How large was the bowl of corn flakes? And why was I drinking water?]

And the correct answer is: Stepnother had poured the milk onto an extra-small bowl of corn flakes. The flakes were soggy and milk-logged according to any means of scientific analysis. Pouring the milk allowed stepnother to meet three important goals: she could be thrifty (DONT WASTE IT IT COSTS MONEY YOU KNOW), she could prevent me from getting sufficient protein and vitamins which would discourage me from growing and developing into a (normal?) adult, and she could stop me from deriving any pleasure from the crispy crunch of cereal. As for the water, orange juice cost too much to serve and was allowed only on special occasions (Christmas, Thanksgiving, certain birthdays) or after half-price sales events (79c a half gallon). No matter when, it was always cut with water anyway. To s t r e t c h it further.

How can I do this? How can I write a (true) sentence that explains what it is like to be cheated and tortured with a small bowl of cereal and a glass of water? There are worse things in the world. Newborn babies in dumpsters, children locked in closets or burned with irons.

Children drowning in irrigation canals.

I ate a spoonful of cereal mush. I was alive, and I was eating (but not by choice) sogged-out cereal. I was alive, and I was drinking (but not by choice) water for breakfast. I was alive, and I was (not by choice) starving.

My brain was on fire.

No one said anything, paid any attention to me. Stepnother was standing at the stove frying an egg for herself. Stepbother Roger was finishing some project for science class. Stepblister Rebecca wanted help fixing her hair. Halfblister Roxie was watching cartoons. I wasn't going to see any of them again.

Emma was eating her cereal. I watched her take a bite. She was happy there. Happy to eat that cereal. Happy to have her F and M (who was really a stepnother). She didn't know any better. And she had years to find out about blisters and bothers and nothers and Fs.

But I already knew.

And I was alive.

Even if everything else was NOT BY CHOICE.

Until today.

Until a perfectly normal December 20th, that no one knew was strange until it was much too late.

On the way back to my bedroom (garage variety), I passed F and stepnother's bedroom. He was sitting on his bed, tying his shoes. His brain was thinking: Normal morning. His brain was thinking: Today will be the same as always. His brain was thinking: JD can't think or feel anything. Then his brain thought: Why am I thinking about JD?

I stood in the doorway.

"What do you want?" F asked.

Already annoyed. All ready for a fight.

"I want to talk."

"I'm late," F said. "I have to drive to Safford."

"I want to talk to you," I said. I shut the bedroom door for privacy.

"I have to finish getting ready," F said and walked into his bathroom.

I edged my way toward the jewelry box. I heard the water running in the bathroom sink. I watched the bathroom door as I touched the jewelry box lid. In a second, I had it open. No one was going to catch me. I was unstoppable. I lifted out the tray and found the stack of green bills. I took them all. They were in my hand when the water stopped. The tray was back, the lid was closed, the bills were in my pocket.

Everything was all right.

Then stepnother walked in.

"What're you doing here with the door closed?" she asked.

"Talking to (I will say it, I told myself, I will say a D-word that's been D for a long time) Dad."

"About what?"

"Yes, about what?" F asked, stepping out of the bathroom.

"About how to get along better," I said. "What can I do to get along better? I've been thinking about it."

"Oh, I'll tell you what you can do," stepnother said. "Stop stealing, stop lying, stop the entire attitude."

My teeth were crunching bone, but I made myself taste chocolate chips.

"Okay," I said.

Stepnother watched me.

"I'd really like to be part of the family," I said.

"Just start acting like part of the family," F said. "You might even get the lock off your door. Do you think your M (I was thinking: notmyM, notmyM, notmyM, notmyM, notmyM) likes to lock you in every night? Do you think it's something she enjoys? Why don't you — okay, I know, you asked what you can do to get along better? You can start by calling her 'M.' Can you do that? Can you do that for me?"

"Sure, I can do that." The words slid out like they were all greased up with butter and my tongue was wax paper. "M," I said, looking at her, "I want to try to get along better."

"Good," she said. "It's about time."

"Yes," I agreed. "It is about time."

I was a liar and a thief. But at least I was going to be a rich one.

"I have your breakfast ready," stepnother told him.

I pretended to go back to my room, but when they had gone to the kitchen, I hurried back to their room, opened the bottom drawer of F's dresser, and removed NB #1.

I took it back to my room. I had hidden a brown paper grocery bag in my closet, and I wanted to put a few shirts in it but I couldn't take the chance. Why would I take a brown paper bag (besides my lunch) to school? What if there was a door check on the way out of the house? So I put my two NBs with my school nbs and my school books.

Then I walked to the door of the room and looked at the lock on the door. I looked at the P can: full and sitting in the middle of the room. I wasn't going to empty it again. I was only going to P in toilets. I looked at all my THINGS on the walls. They would throw them out — or rip them up. But it didn't matter. I could make THINGS anywhere.

I walked out and shut the door.

"I'm leaving," I called. What did they know? They didn't know what those two words meant.

"Goodbye," I said. They didn't know how different that word sounded to me this time.

I didn't wait for an answer.

What would they say?

a. "Have a good day."
b. "Come here and kiss me goodbye."
c. "I love you."

Every answer was wrong. The test was failed. No hope for passing this class. I closed the front door and started walking.

I never even looked back.

CHAPTER TWO

THE PLACE (WHERE I AM GOING)

A ghost walked down a Tempe street. Its feet floated over the sidewalk. It was practically invisible. Anyone who tried to stop it would not be able to grasp its body at all. It was unstoppable. It was the only unreal thing in a real world.

Surprise! It was me.

But then I stopped being a ghost. I stopped being an unreal thing and became the only real thing in an unreal world. My eyes couldn't see anything real. Not the sidewalk cracks, not the dead ocotillos. Not the blue sky (no clouds). Not the irrigation control station.

At the next corner I turned and looked at S's house. I hadn't seen her since Saturday night. She might be inside waiting to come out. She might see me.

She might not.

I was gambling. I wanted to see her. I wanted her to know what I was doing. I wanted to say: Goodbye, it'll be all right. Find another friend that you can talk to, that you can share your secrets with. I want to know you (and be your friend) but I have to get some fresh (free) air or I'll D. Have a good life. But I didn't want her to know where I was going. What if they asked her? What if she talked?

I started walking. I got to the corner of Hardy and University and headed down University. In a few minutes I passed the high school, but I didn't stop there. At any moment, my eyes expected F to drive up and ask what I was doing. But my brain knew better: why would he ever check on me? (I wasn't worth checking on.) I was always locked away somewhere: school, my bedroom. There was no reason to think that I would escape.

As soon as I was past the high school, I felt safe in a new way. There were no locks beyond the high school. I was almost at Arizona State where I was going to meet Jesus and his friends.

I had found Jesus Martinez on a ride board at the ASU union. The ride board was a map of the United States. Every state had a hook. Students who wanted a ride or drivers who wanted passengers could hang a notice on the state they wanted a ride to. I couldn't put a notice up. I didn't have an address or a telephone number.

I wasn't a real person.

But Jesus was.

He wasn't even going to Wheeling, West Virginia. He was going to Pittsburgh, but when I called him he said yes, he would be passing through Wheeling on the interstate. Yes, I could ride with him. He would split the cost with me and his friends. Maybe $50. We would drive straight through. Could I drive? I lied. Yes, I said, I drive.

"Do you go to ASU?" he asked me.

"Yes," the liar said.

"What year?"

"Freshman," the liar answered.

"So am I," he said. "What's your phone number?"

"Oh, well, this is kind of a surprise," the liar continued. "I don't want anyone to know. You can't call me at home."

"Then how do I know you'll show up?"

"I'll call you," the liar promised. "Every day if you want."

"Okay," he said, "call me tomorrow."

So the liar called him every day for a week, and when he wasn't in his dorm room, the liar left messages.

"This is for Jesus," the liar said. "Tell him that Julian called."

The liar wasn't sure he was going. The liar wasn't sure he had the courage. Then certain things happened; choices were made. The liar was telling Jesus the truth after all.

Jesus said to meet him at 9:00 WA, and I wasn't going to be late. As I walked across Mill Avenue, the sun was so bright I felt sick. My stomach squeezed itself tight.

That's when I decided to dump my school books and nbs (but save my NBs). I couldn't carry them another foot. I don't know what it looked like to throw perfectly good (but bad) books away. My brain wondered: What would I do if someone asked me what I was doing? Oh, I would say, I must have accidentally dropped them in the LITTER STOPS HERE barrel.

But no one saw or (if they did) said anything.

Jesus said, "Where's your suitcase?"

"I'm a walking suitcase," the liar joked.

He didn't understand.

"Do you have your money?" he asked.

"I'm also a walking bank," the liar said. Or maybe a bank robber.

As I got in the car with his two friends, he said, "Why don't you give me $20 now for the first tank of gas?"

He didn't trust me.

"Sure," I said. I pulled out my wallet and looked at all my money for the first time. I had some McMoney and lots more stepnother money. Altogether, I had

$535 in my wallet and 14 cents in my pocket. I couldn't imagine having more money; I was rich. I could go to school for over fifteen years almost on this milk money.

Or I could make sure I got to Wheeling — and beyond.

"Here's $40," I said.

Jesus and his friends drove the car crackling and sizzling down the interstates like we were a fuse on a bomb. Flagstaff, Albuquerque, Amarillo, Oklahoma City, Wichita, Kansas City, St. Louis. Express. It was like taking my trip from West Virginia to Arizona with F and stepnother backwards. All the towns, all the miles, all the memories were burning up, as Jesus and his friends drove us backwards to Wheeling. I kept checking your watch to make sure it was running forward. When Jesus asked me to drive, I said I felt sick. He didn't argue.

We stopped for gas every 300 miles or so. We stopped for food when the driver was hungry. We stopped to sleep three times. The rest of the time we were driving.

The first place we stopped to sleep was Amarillo. John (a friend of Jesus) stopped along a strip of side road filled with tourist places and everyone slept. Except me. I couldn't sleep, so I got (q u i e t l y) out of the car. I walked along the street in front of us, covering ground we were going to drive. There were sleeping restaurants, dozing gas stations, drowsy motels. I walked for blocks, looking at the sky, filled with a big moon and a thousand stars.

The stars asked me:

Were F and stepnother C? (smile)

Were they laughing?

Did they call the police (as a formality)?

Did Roger move his couch into the GB?

Would Emma understand?

And did it matter?

The stars told me this was the first night that I could sleep unlocked. I was unlocked.

And then I saw the motel. The Ghost Ranch. It loomed in front of me like a monument, a mausoleum. Stolen, under cover of darkness, by conniving thieves and child abusers, and transported from West Virginia to Arizona, I had stopped there once. I had slept there once.

Now my eyes looked in the window under the red Vacancy sign and saw an old man. My eyes had seen him when we had stopped at the Ghost Ranch before.

Only now he was older. My brain would never have remembered him, would never have remembered anything at all. Except the past was in front of my eyes.

I wasn't supposed to tell anyone who we were or where we had come from or anything about us. And I had. I had chosen him.

I needed to get ice for their drinks. I had taken the bucket, but I couldn't find the ice machine. And I asked the old man.

Maybe he was like Mrs. Pope. Maybe he wasn't. But he sensed something.

"You're moving out West?" he asked.

"Yes," he said.

"Where to?"

"Arizona."

"Where are you coming from?"

I told him and then he said:

"I bet your friends were sad to see you leave."

They didn't know we were leaving. They didn't know anything at all. I wasn't a liar (or a thief) then. So I told him. About the darkness. About the streetlight. About the sadness.

And when my eyes looked up, stepnother was there, her ears doing rabbit twitches, her eyes playing ping-pong.

"I wondered where you got to," she said. "Now where's that ice machine?"

Her nails punctured my shirt and skin on the way back to the room. My eyes were C, but my mouth couldn't scream.

"I'll teach you to talk," she said. "I'll teach you to tell things."

She unwrapped the Ghost Ranch soap. It was a bar of golden Dial. She lathered it up. My brain thought it was going to be used on my hands, my face. It couldn't imagine anything else.

Only she took the lathery soap and shoved it in my mouth and pressed it so hard that my lips were cut and bleeding and bubbles slid down my throat. I was gagging and choking. And I thought I would D right then and there. But I didn't. I only threw up my dinner.

F was watching from the doorway.

"Get down and clean up your mess," F said. "You'd better have more common sense in the future."

My brain asked itself questions: The common sense to keep my mouth closed to stop soap from being shoved down my throat? Or the common sense to keep my mouth closed to stop words from falling out?

Then my brain chose a mouth that could not produce many words. My brain chose a mouth that was shut and soap-protected (mostly).

But sometimes a mouth has a life of its own.

It was snowing in Wheeling when Jesus stopped. 7:08 WP. December 23.

"I'm not pulling off the highway," he said. "I don't want to get stuck."

"Okay."

"This looks like the downtown exit."

A yellow tunnel (and Pittsburgh) was staring at us. A plunging exit road led to downtown Wheeling.

And you.

It was bad weather. The snowflakes were fat and fluffy and piling high.

"Thanks," I said to everyone. "Bye."

CHAPTER THREE
NO PLANS (ANYTHING GOES)

I had no specific plan as I walked down the slippery exit into Wheeling. I had spent three days thinking about possibilities and three days unable to decide. I knew why I had come to Wheeling (to find you) and I had memorized what to do next (go, surround, isolate, wait, and pray for bad weather) — but how and where and when were all too confusing.

All I was thinking about was the slippery road and the exit ramp. What if a car skidded out of control and hit me? What if I D on my way into Wheeling? What if

But I reached the bottom of the ramp. Alive. Without plans.

Alone.

Maybe I was stupid; stepnother always thought so. Maybe my brain couldn't think of anything else. But as I walked down Main Street in Wheeling, past old (and familiar) buildings, near the Suspension Bridge and the Capitol Theatre, I knew where I could stay. What I mean is: I knew where a liar and a thief could spend the night.

After we had moved to Arizona, our West Virginia house had been sold to the Raymonds. Roberta Raymond had been in my class. I used to play chess with her sometimes. I used to eat spaghetti at her house on nights that you were too sick to cook. The Raymonds had a small old house. Roberta's mother thought she looked like Michelle Pfeiffer and needed a bigger house. So when the house was put up for sale after we made our dark exit, the Raymonds bought it.

"Hello, is Roberta there?"

"Who's calling, please?"

A liar and a thief, my brain thought.

"Julian Drew," I said. "Is this Mr. Raymond?"

"Julian? Are you in town?"

"Actually, yes," I said. "I'm on my way to visit my grandmother in Pittsburgh, and the bus broke down. I'm short on money, and I was wondering if I could spend the night."

"Well, of course. You know where we're at. Can you get yourself over here? Or do you need a ride?"

"No, I can get there," I said.

I don't know what I expected when I knocked on the door.

No, that's another lie. I do know. I expected to go back five or six years. I expected you (YOU) to open the door. I expected you to look at me and say:

"Where have you been? Your F and I were so worried. You look like you're soaked to the bone. Get in here, Julian, and take those wet things off. Your F just put the tree up. You can help him decorate it. I'm going to make hot chocolate and popcorn."

I expected the house would have the same furniture, the same plants, the same paint, the same pictures, the same toilet paper, the same breaths and heartbeats.

I expected you (my M), and I got the Raymonds instead. Their house was not our old house. It was wallpapered with ducks and drums and filled with artificial flowers. It had different smells and unfamiliar air.

Roberta Raymond was tall and thin now; she was old enough that my memory of her was all wrong. Only Michelle Pfeiffer and her husband looked the same.

"Where's your suitcase?" Mr. Raymond asked.

"It's in the bus. They said we could leave it there. I just brought myself."

All I carried were my notebooks.

"What'd you do? Bring your homework?" Mr. Raymond asked. "Why don't you put those upstairs? Roberta, you can show Julian where."

Without a word, Roberta led me to my old bedroom.

But it wasn't my bedroom anymore. I sat on the

bed, but the mattress was hard and not the kind of place where you would sit and tell me stories. The windows were covered with thick curtains, not the gauzy ones that let me look at the sky each night.

I talked and talked and lied and lied to the Raymonds. But all I felt like doing was C.

When I went to bed, I opened the curtains and turned out the light and stared hard at my closet door. I had left it wide open. The room was dark, the closet doorway darker. This was the one place I always thought I'd see a ghost. I never thought it would be your ghost. I never thought you would D. And I stared and stared at the closet doorway that night. Trying to make ghost shapes out of clothes, trying to make your shape out of darkness.

But there was nothing to form. You weren't there anymore. The feel of you had moved out. My insides felt more lost and lonely than they had been. I tried to sleep an old warm sleep, a sleep with happy dreams of you. But there were no dreams in that house and no real sleep, because there was no you.

The next morning the snow had stopped. A beautiful Christmas Eve. And time to go.

"Do you want to call the bus station?" Mr. Raymond asked.

"I already did," I lied. "I've got to get there by 9:30."

"Then I'll give you a ride."

At the station, a little later, he said, "Are you sure you'll be okay? Would you like me to wait a while just to make sure?"

"No," I told him, "Jesus got me this far. Somehow I'll manage the rest of the way."

"What a fine Christian boy you are," he said. "If you're ever passing through again, you stop and see us. Tell your family hello."

He didn't know that this fine Christian boy had taken a bar of soap and a half-empty bottle of shampoo.

I waited a few minutes and, when I was sure that he had gone, I left the bus station. Maybe you weren't at the old house anymore. But you had to be in town. I would find you. And I was going to find a place to stay. Not a hotel: too much money and too many eyes. Maybe an apartment.

I could walk in any direction. I could go anywhere I chose. I wasn't sure how to choose or which way was best, but then my feet took charge. They turned south and I found myself walking past the old B&O station, walking toward Weirton. Then I started to see signs (Ohio Valley General Hospital) and arrows (←) and my feet followed them.

But why were my feet going there? I never visited you at the hospital. I never knew anything about it except that you were taken there to have operations and then to D.

My feet turned the corner at 12th Street, and my eyes could see the hospital up the hill. Then my feet turned another corner and walked along Market Square. There were stores and restaurants. And I was tired and hungry and the $473.72 in my pocket wanted to help me.

I found myself in front of a store called Grandma's Attic.

"You made it just in time," Grandma said. "I was thinking about closing at noon for Christmas Eve. Can I help you find something?"

I probably looked strange. A stranger in a strange place. A junkman in a junkhouse.

My brain was thinking.

"I want a sunflower pitcher," I said.

"Roseville?" she asked.

I didn't know what she meant.

"Roseville was the name of a pottery that made sunflower pitchers. Is that what you want?"

"I don't know."

She said, "I think I picked one up at an estate sale last week. Come on over here. It's in one of these boxes."

About a dozen cardboard boxes were pushed into the far corner. Each was filled with balls of crumpled newspaper. She started unwrapping each ball. "No . . . no . . . no . . ." she said as she unwrapped each item. "Here it is. Well, you may not want it."

"Why?"

She handed me the pitcher. It was yellow, with a golden sunflower. It looked like your pitcher.

"The spout is chipped. It's pretty beat up."

"How much is it?"

"If it was in good shape, I could get sixty, maybe seventy for it. I'll give it to you for twenty."

I wanted that pitcher to be mine (even with a chip) but my eyes needed to see more things. "I want to look around," I said.

"Tell you what," Grandma said. "I'll give it to you for fifteen, but that's my best offer. That's a Christmas special."

"I want it," I told her. "But I want to look around first."

"Go right ahead," she said. "I'll keep the pitcher right here for you. Why don't you start with the top floor? See anything you want, just bring it down."

As the elevator door opened on the top floor, my eyes saw gloom and dust and my nose smelled years of rainwater leaks. I walked by stacks of old furniture. Now I was a homing pigeon. My feet had delivered me to the store. Suddenly, I was flying (not walking) to a home I didn't know existed. I made my way past wobbly tables and chairs with cracked leather seats. I saw kitchen cupboards with chipped enamel counters. I was heading straight for the back of the store where bookcases lined the wall.

As soon as I parked myself in front of the bookcases, I realized that I had stood here once before. Not in Grandma's Attic, but in my dream. In my nowhere dream. I had dreamed about this place, I had dreamed about a bookcase. Now things were sharper. Now I knew where I was.

And I looked straight ahead at a five-shelf bookcase. One shelf — and no others — held a row of books. My eyes stared at the books. There were ten books on the shelf, but I only knew one: Portrait of Jennie.

I picked up the book.

My hands were shaking.

I opened it slowly.

I thought it might crumble into dust.

But my brain — my dream memory — knew what I would find.

Your name was written inside.

And the letter — the letter I had nowhere-dreamed about — was waiting inside the back cover.

Jan 31
Tues aft
3:20 p.m.

Dear Mom,

I am here and settled. I don't know what this is going to be like. I've never been on my own before but I think it will be all right. Who knows? Maybe it will even all work out fine.

I like Wheeling. Everyone is so friendly. All you have to do is look at someone and they nearly talk your leg off. Of course, I look so young and probably seem so alone that they feel a little sorry for me.

I know you don't want to know this, but I'll write it anyway. Drew came to visit last Friday. He got here at 9; he said he would be here early and he was right. He was a little peeved that I was waiting for him in the lobby. He told me I should've waited in the apartment, but I was so excited to have my first company (even him) that I stood there for half an hour waiting to see his car. I'm hardly an invalid.

Now that I've told you this much, I'll give you the rest: he asked me to marry him. I know I shouldn't believe him after everything. And I know you won't want me to marry him. BUT (as you've always said — and probably regretted) it's my life and I've got to do what makes me happy. I'm just sorry that this whole thing has made you unhappy. Maybe things will work out. (Oops — I think I've said that twice now. I guess I'm just a permanent optimist!)

I didn't say yes, and I didn't say no. I just said I'd think about it. My brain is working on this one. I don't want to make any mistakes this time around. Will you ever forgive me if I say yes? Will you ever forgive me if I don't?

With love,
Your (very confused) Jenny

The letter was dated twenty years ago. You had addressed it to your mother in Parkersburg. Your return address was in the top left corner of the envelope: Jenny Sayre, 93 Market Street, Apt. 3, Wheeling, WVa.

I was standing still on the top floor of Grandma's Attic. But I was traveling, traveling in time. My body was on a backwards trip through a nowhere dream.

The envelope had a stamp, but it had never been canceled. For some reason, you had put it in the book and never mailed it.

Why? To save it for me?

And what were you doing in Wheeling? Why weren't you married? You always told me that you had moved to Wheeling with F when you got married. Was that a lie?

I bought the book ($1) and pitcher ($15) and never mentioned the letter (in my pocket). Then I was outside, walking back to town. Now I knew exactly where I was going.

I headed up Market Street reading numbers on old brick buildings. 142 Market had a vacancy. 130 and 122 Market had no vacancies. But it didn't matter. I kept walking. There was only one place to go.

It was snowing again. Heavy. Traffic was light. I kept on thinking: BAD WEATHER (and smiling).

This was the kind of day to go traveling.

Then my eyes saw a Vacancy sign at 93 Market.

The manager said, "Apartment 7 is vacant."

"What about Apartment 3?" I asked.

He looked surprised. "That's taken," he said. "Look, it's $80 a week and another $80 for the security deposit. That includes utilities. It's Christmas Eve and I'm busy. You want to see it?"

"Yes," I said.

He asked some questions on the way upstairs: did I have a roommate, was I working, how old was I.

"I'm twenty," I said. "I have a job. And I have money."

I was surprised but he didn't ask any more questions.

Apartment 7 was small. A living room/kitchen, a bathroom, and a bedroom. Small rooms, old wood floors, dirty walls. The kitchen had an old stove and refrigerator, a chipped enamel sink. It was perfect.

I gave him money for the deposit and one week's rent and got the key.

I didn't feel you in the apartment, even though Apartment 3 was down the hall on the right. But I had a sunflower pitcher, your book, and your letter. It could still be your home. And I could stand in the lobby where you stood in the lobby.

I was hungry, so I went out to find a grocery store. Two blocks down was a convenience market. I bought milk and plastic cups and two loaves of bread. As soon as I got home (Apartment 7 <u>was</u> home now) I washed the sunflower pitcher and filled it with milk. Then I poured the milk into a plastic cup and drank it.

I will never forget the taste. It was sweet and cold and filled with memories.

It was like getting a transfusion of you.

CHAPTER FOUR
THE WIND BLOWS, THE SEA FLOWS

I couldn't stay alone in empty rooms on Christmas Eve, so I decided to go SHOPPING! I knew just what to BUY. I couldn't find any 2×4s but I found five cinder blocks in an alley (not far away) and took them to my home. Then I went back for an old Formica countertop propped up on someone's back fence. The Formica was peeling away, but it was wide enough for me. I chose a space by the hottest radiator and put one cinder block under each corner and another in the middle. Then I covered the countertop with some old newspapers I had found in the front hall of the apartment building.

Now I was ready for bed on Christmas Eve. I took a bath and washed my hair with Roberta Raymond's shampoo. I didn't have a towel so I used the dirtiest undershirt to dry myself. Then I finished the sunflower milk and climbed into bed. I used my jacket as a blanket. I was going to have to be very flexible. I knew that.

I got up early Christmas morning. The nice thing about sleeping in my clothes was that I didn't have to get dressed. For breakfast, I drank some water (my sunflower milk was gone) and finished one loaf of bread. My brain wasn't thinking much about Christmas.

I went walking. I knew where my feet were going this time. I had already been to our house. Now I had someplace to go. I walked down National Road and past the Big Boy and by the Presbyterian church. I heard the choir singing; they sounded like angels. But I kept walking up Chicken Neck Hill and down. Then I passed by the Methodist church and made my way up another hill.

My shoes were wet from slushy sidewalks. The tip of my nose and my toes were freezing. But I kept going up the hill.

You were waiting for me at Greenwood. I used to go there every day after you D. I would sit on top of you and ask you to appear. Sometimes I even took a nap on you. I couldn't leave you once I got there. I would take you flowers. One time I clipped all of Mrs. Jasper's chrysanthemums. I was mad at stepnother and just took a knife and cut the mums and brought them to you. I thought it would bring you back to me. I thought you would wake up and smell them. It was just another time that I was wrong.

But there you were: Jennifer Sayre Drew. I was standing on you, Christmas Day, watching for any sign that you were near. I hadn't seen you since the afternoon of the night we left. Then your grass was brown and filled with busy ants. Now you were covered with snow and you looked cold. In Memoriam, the stone said (and still says). In Memoriam doesn't even come close.

I wondered where and how I could arrange to see you. I wasn't going to find you in our old house or at Greenwood. I wasn't going to find you in Apartment 7, even if you had lived down the hall. Wherewhere-where? Then my brain thought: what about the lobby? What about the lobby on January 27th? You were waiting in the downstairs hall for F to show up from 8:30 to 9:00. I could wait there on the morning of January 27th and intercept you.

But how could I do this? My brain repeated: GO, SURROUND, ISOLATE, WAIT, and PRAY FOR BAD WEATHER. I had already GONE (from Arizona to West Virginia) and I was trying to SURROUND, but I needed more than a book and a sunflower pitcher. And I needed more than $289.84 to do it. I needed $320 to pay the rent until January 28th. I was going to have to try harder. And maybe I would have to get some McMoney.

My brain was so busy and you weren't saying a word. Just staring up at me, so peaceful and quiet. Except for the wind howling through the evergreens.

My breath was forming steam-puffs.

I bit my lips and waved goodbye. And then my feet were walking away from you.

The next morning (Monday, December 26) I went shopping again at Grandma's Attic.

Since my money wasn't going to go far enough to fill the apartment, I decided to fill the kitchen. I found a kitchen table with metal legs, a Formica top, and two chairs ($60), a broken transistor radio ($5), a tablecloth with roses ($5), four glasses like the ones we used for iced tea ($10), 2 plates ($10), wooden spoons and a spatula with a green wood handle ($4), some old candles ($3), and a chipped and glued mixing bowl with blue stripes that looked just like one of yours ($12).

Everything came to $109, but the woman let me have it for $70. She said they would even deliver everything to me that afternoon for another $10.

I was down to $209.84. And there was rent to pay.

First I needed clothes, so I took a bus to Sunnyside and shopped at Kmart: two shirts, a 3-pack of underwear and detergent for $21.47. DONT SAY I NEVER BOUGHT YOU ANYTHING. On the way there I saw a Hostess Thrift Shop so I stopped on the way back and bought two shopping bags full of stale bread.

I went home to Apartment 7, filled myself full and cleaned myself up.

Afterwards, I went to the downtown McD's. I asked for an application and filled it out with lies. We had just moved to town. We didn't have a phone. I was over eighteen. I listed my previous experience and the equipment I could operate.

At the bottom, I wrote: "I like to mop floors."

I got the job on the spot: 40 hours a week, starting Wednesday. No questions asked, except I needed something to prove that I was 18. I said my birth certificate was coming in the moving van, and I would bring it in a few days. The McManager agreed. Then I went home to wait for my kitchen.

After the truck left, I put everything away. I turned on my broken transistor radio (golden light but no sound). Then I poured a glass of sunflower milk and sat at my table (with tablecloth) and pretended I was sitting there twenty years ago. You were down the hall. You were the beautiful girl I had seen walking into the building. You were not my M.

And I wondered how I could get to know you. Could I stop you in the hallway and introduce myself? Could I slip a note under your door? Could I meet you walking up Market Street and accompany you home? Could I talk to you about your favorite books? Could I talk to you about Portrait of Jennie?

Or would I meet you on the morning of January 27th when you waited for F (who was not my F then) twenty years ago?

Would you realize that I had traveled through time to find you?

I paid my rent for two more weeks and started to work, 6:00 WA to 2:30 WP. For three weeks I got up in the morning, put on my clothes, and walked to McDonald's. I mopped, I cleaned toilets, I volunteered for every job. I did them all with a smile. I only had $49.32 (and no payday in sight) so I ate as much McFood as I could at work. And bread (half a loaf every day) at home. When I walked home after work, I tried to ISOLATE. But after seeing plastic seats and cardboard signs, after smelling Egg McMuffins and Big Macs, I couldn't get my mind into the past.

On Friday, January 13th, the fifteenth work morning (which was also my first payday) I went to work, got paid for ten days ($241.77), said I was sick, and left. After I paid the rent through January 28th, I had exactly $82.03 total. Stepnother's money had run out; McMoney was running out. But I didn't care. All I was thinking about was the morning of January 27th and how I was going to meet you. I was never going back to McD's again.

For the next week, I lived a different life. I slept during the day and stayed up all night. At night, I could make believe that I had begun to go backwards. I would wake up at 7:00 WP and think about you until midnight. I would eat bread and milk. Then I went outside and walked down Main Street to Market Square, then up Market Street and over the hill to National Road. As soon as I could, I would turn onto side streets and avoid the main road. Too much neon, too many cars.

I would walk as far as our old house and pretend it was years ago. I walked like this: I closed my eyes and walked ten steps (if I thought it was safe — no corners, no sidewalk cracks). I told myself I was going backwards. I told myself you might be there. I pictured an invisible barrier, like a door frame, and I imagined stepping over it into the past. I did this on every block, on every walk, every night after I quit working at McD's.

On the main road, I would look in trash cans if the coast was clear. I didn't want the police to stop me (not that anyone was looking for me). My face wasn't going to appear on local (or even faraway) milk cartons. I didn't have to talk to or be with anyone, except when I bought groceries at 5:00 WA on the way back to the apartment.

One night I walked to my old school, Steenrod. You weren't there, but everything about me was. The playgrounds where I had played, the rooms where I had learned arithmetic and parts of speech and syllabication, the principal's office. He had called you one day to say that I was sick and needed to come home early. I remember that day because you were going to the hospital soon and I was worried and I needed you (but you sent me to school).

Even at night I could see that the windows of each classroom were decorated with construction paper cutouts of red Santas or black sleighs or white snowflakes or green candles with yellow flames or brown bags of toys. The teachers had used the same patterns when I had been there, four (and more) years before. Everything looked the same, only I was older and not part of Steenrod anymore, not part of any life in Wheeling anymore. Except yours.

The last night I walked, January 20th, I came back to Market Street at 5:19 WA when it was 42 degrees according to the Wheeling Dollar time and temperature clock. I walked to the Suspension Bridge and stopped halfway across. No one was there. The bridge felt like the oldest thing in town. The river was foggy and my eyes couldn't make out any boats. I sat there and leaned against the railing and thought.

Thoughts fill a brain.

Thoughts feel so real, but they're like smoke. They just disappear. I thought about you. Why you were living in Wheeling before you got married. Why you married F after all. Why you had always said that you got married and then moved to Wheeling.

My brain knew before I did. My brain knew a math problem:

> If a boy is 16 and his M was pregnant 20 years ago, who was the baby and what happened to it? Bonus points for determining exactly when and where the M got married. Record your answer in the space below and show the steps you used to reach your solution.

This was a problem my Arizona brain wouldn't have liked, a problem my Arizona brain would have wanted to forget. But my West Virginia brain liked this problem and started thinking thoughts. What would have happened if you hadn't married F? Would you have been happy (happier)? Would you have stayed healthy (healthier)?

Then my West Virginia brain produced the biggest thought of all: what would happen if I traveled to your time on January 27th and took you away before F showed up? Would it be possible to live together — you, the then-baby, and the now-me? Would it be possible to be our own special then-and-now family? My brain was tired of thinking about possibilities, it wanted to think about Things that Can, that Will. Things that Are.

Sitting on the Suspension Bridge ISOLATED from noise and SURROUNDED by foggy BAD WEATHER made my brain think this could be done. But not by walking all night. I was going to have to use more drastic measures. I was going to have to make more sacrifices. How could I travel back to you if I didn't ISOLATE and purify myself of everything in the present? My brain knew that I could walk to the moon and back in a tornado and you weren't going to appear on January 27th. Leaving McDonald's wasn't enough. Walking all night wasn't enough either. Nothing from today could be on or in my body. Everything would have to be more than twenty years old.

And then my brain made a plan:

My body couldn't leave the apartment. My mouth couldn't drink milk from the sunflower pitcher (it was from new cows). It couldn't eat bread (it was from new wheat). It couldn't eat any food. But what about tap water? Was it old or new? My brain said: nothing new or travel can't be done.

Maybe my mouth could have water. It came down the river, went to the ocean, and was turned into rain. Water was as old as the earth. But nothing else.

Nothing else.

Except the right clothes. That morning I broke my rule for the only time and went out in sunlight. I found an old clothing store called Mary's Closet five stores down from Grandma's Attic and bought a sweater, some wool pants, a starchy white shirt, and a tie. There were no socks or underwear. There were no shoes. I paid $25. Everything was at least 20 years old. Mary told me so.

But my brain decided to eliminate temptation. At 11:14 WA I walked halfway across the Suspension

Bridge. It was still foggy and the bridge was empty. I took the rest of my McMoney and threw it into the foggy river. I didn't need to eat or buy anything. I just needed to prepare myself for you.

CHAPTER FIVE
NOBODY KNOWS

I cleaned the apartment.

I threw my Arizona clothes away. No more jacket, no more shoes, no more socks or underwear. I put on my new (old) clothes: brown pants (a little baggy), the shirt (sleeves a little too long), the tie (tied wrong), and sweater (perfect fit). I didn't have much heat, but my feet didn't seem to notice after a while.

I threw away my newspaper bed and my last loaf of bread. The only new things I kept were my NBs, which I hid behind the toilet.

For six days and nights I slept or walked the perimeter of the apartment. I kept the shades pulled and only lit a candle (using the gas burner) when I needed to see. I was a ghost now. No one saw me go in or go out, because I went nowhere. I was in nowhere time, not new, not old. Just nowhere time, and I was waiting, waiting for January 27th. 8:30 WA. I read Portrait of Jennie when I could and I read your letter over and over again. I traced your handwriting with my finger. I memorized every word. You had waited for F for half an hour. You wrote that he had gotten there at nine.

So 8:30 WA it would be. I was going to cut F off at the pass.

That whole week, my body grew thinner than it already was. My stomach gnawed, but it was no different than living with stepnother. I knew how to live on almost nothing. The ache was like my only friend, but then it stopped. Sometimes my head felt heavy and my eyes were dizzy.

By the morning of January 27th I had to hold on to stand up. But I didn't care.

The morning of January 27th SOUNDED promising. I couldn't look, but I heard raindrops pat against my windows.

BAD WEATHER.

I sat in the kitchen chair and kept track of the time on your watch. I turned on the transistor radio. The dial lit like always, but no music played. I was too tired to move. I remember at 7:03 WA I put my head on the table and almost fell asleep. At 8:15 WA I took the radio and started to make my way to the door. I knew it would take a while.

I leaned on the railing and moved slowly down the steps. I heard cars splashing in the rain outside. I kept wishing they would sound different, older somehow. I made it to the bottom of the stairs and turned the corner. I needed to think about this. I needed to think about you. I needed to picture you in the building twenty years earlier. And I needed to do it without being interrupted.

So I sat in the space under the staircase. No one could see me there if I leaned up against the wall. The hallway was dark. Only daylight or streetlight lit it. I tried to hold my arm up to keep watching the time. But it wouldn't stay.

My brain wondered how it would know if you were coming. Would there be footsteps on the stairs when you left your apartment and came down to wait? Had you been out (buying a paper, taking a walk) and come through the front door? The stairs? The door? My brain kept repeating: stairsdoorstairsdoor.

8:30 WA and no noises. Just cars driving through the rain. My ears were ready: footstepsonthestairs or doorknobturning. But my eyes were ready to sleep.

Suddenly there was the sound of a door closing upstairs and someone walking down the hall. I could tell that they were coming from the third floor. I could hear the clickclick of high heels. I could tell it was the third floor lady with the green coat and airplane pin.

I wasn't trying hard enough.

My brain said: gobackbackback and picturepicture your M. Youcanmeether, youcanmeether. But my brain was too overloaded to work and it was nine, then after nine, and I felt sicker than ever.

But my brain had an idea: Why 9:00 WA? Why not 9:00 WP? What if F had come at night? What if you had started waiting at 8:30 WP?

I didn't know if I could believe this. But there wouldn't be anymore chances. January 27th: 8:30 WP. Okay, I thought, okay. One more chance.

But I couldn't move and I tried to stretch my sweater far enough down to cover my bare toes. It was cold in the hall under the stairs. And my eyes just wanted to shut.

It's okay, I told myself, you can sleep. You can sleep until your M comes at 8:30 WP.

So my eyes closed and when they opened, they saw darkness. I was lost in a black place and I forgot where I was. I tried to sit up and hit my head on the ceiling under the stairs. Then I wondered (worried) what time it was. It couldn't be after nine.

I crawled out into the hallway and held your watch in the shaft of streetlight that fell through the window in the door. I had to get it close to my eyes. It was 8:40 WP. I had slept too long and nothing was right.

I couldn't even move. I put my head on the hallway floor and felt tears.

Then my ears heard the silence. No cars driving by. No outside noises. Not even inside noises. I turned my head to look at the front door. Why was it so quiet? Could it (I wondered) could I have (I wanted to think), but the questions were afraid to form.

I squeezed my eyes almost closed and focused on the window in the front door. What was happening? Or was anything happening. Was I just imagining that everything was different?

Then I saw it: snow. Snow was making everything quiet. Snow was swallowing the noises and cars and people and eating them whole. It was just snow.

I was stupid, my brain was thinking, wasting money and time and most of all me for something that wasn't possible. Something that could never work. Something that was NOTHING. If I was with F and stepnother I would be better, wouldn't I? I would be eating, wouldn't I? But I would be locked in.

Locked in once and locked in twice. Arizona or West Virginia. Locked in everywhere. I was out of money and only had a place to stay for one more night. I didn't know what I was going to do. My brain couldn't really think or make plans right then.

I don't know why, really, except maybe my brain thought it was my last chance. But I felt for my transistor radio and turned it on. The dial lit with a yellow glow. Then maybe because I was mad or maybe because I was so weak — I dropped it. It crackled after it hit the floor and the dial light flickered and I heard static and then music, but not now-music, then-music. There was then-music filling the hallway, and everything else was quiet.

I looked at the front door window again, expecting to see snow. Only this time there were two gingerbread shadows covered with sticky black honey standing outside the window. They had chocolate chip eyes but they weren't looking at me. And instead of silence I could hear them talking.

"I thought you were never going to get here," the gingerbread woman said.

"The roads were terrible," the gingerbread man said. "You shouldn't have been standing on your feet this long."

"I wanted to see you."

"Have you thought about — "

"Yes, but I don't want to talk about it out here on the sidewalk."

"I was figuring we could get married this weekend. If you — "

"Okay," gingerbread woman said. "I didn't want to get started out here, but I will if that's how you want it. All I know right now is that I don't want to make any decisions. I don't know what I want to do, I don't know what I want to do about the baby, and I don't know what I want to do about you. I'm not making any plans to get married now. I want to have the baby and think about it. Maybe I won't keep the baby. Maybe we'll get married, or maybe not. But I'm not getting roped in anymore than I already am. And I'm not going to change my mind about this no matter how many times you ask."

"Maybe I should just leave. You don't want me for anything."

"Who said that? Weren't you listening? Anyway, it's too late to drive home now. Don't you want to come in?"

"All right," gingerbread man said. "Let me get my things out of the car."

"Meet me upstairs," she said.

The shadows moved away and everything was quiet again. Except for the gasp of the front door opening. The shaft of streetlight widened enough that I could see the time: 9:00 WP. When I looked up, I saw a shadow standing in the doorway.

A gingerbread shadow standing there looking at me.

I must have looked pretty strange. Lying across the hallway, almost passed out, staring at the door.

"Who's there?" the shadow called.

My mouth wasn't working.

Then the shadow moved toward me.

"What are you doing?" it asked.

I couldn't answer.

"Julian?"

I looked up from the floor. Then-music was playing and the shadow was standing over me. And it was saying: "Julian? Oh, Julian! Are you okay? It's me. I came to find you."

I squinted in the darkness and stared hard and the shadow became . . .

CHAPTER SIX
AND WHERE WE ARE GOING

The stairs and the hallway were gone, the apartment building had disappeared. My eyes were closed, but I could see (and not see) another place, hear (and not hear) another world. Wherever I was, it was white and glowing and warm. My brain began to think I had been beamed into the most wonderful UFO. I wasn't afraid of the aliens either.

I could hear a thump, a beat, the second hand of YOUR WATCH ticking its real time. I could hear the beat, the heartbeat of

YOU YOU YOU YOU YOU YOU YOU
YOU YOU YOU YOU YOU YOU
YOU YOU YOU YOU YOU YOU YOU

YOUR HEARTBEAT was so close to my ears and made me feel so safe. My eyes sensed you there, hovering over me (not exactly an angel, more like a butterfly), wrapping my body in the softest silk cocoon and filling my veins with the sweetest liquids. I was floating in that white UFO room, completely surrounded and protected.

And you were talking to me.

"Julian," you said, "can you hear me? I came to find you. I made a big mistake. I guess I should just say it: I got pregnant. I told my mother but all she did was scream at me. She was going to take me out of school and send me somewhere. I couldn't stand it so I ran away. Just like you. I thought that coming to Wheeling might help. I could be on my own. And I knew I could find you here. And you were here. I found you. I FOUND YOU."

And you smelled like you and touched like you and breathed every breath like you. I kept floating, but I was afraid you were going to disappear. So I tried to say "But what about?" and "How can we?" But you placed your fingers on my lips and shhhed me and made everything okay.

Finally, I slept for a long time and saw nothing except a creamy darkness. I could feel you beside me. You were like a dark sun radiating strength and healing, but no glare. When my sleep was over, my eyes wanted to open (knowing that now they were ready to see again). They blinked and focused on the shadow that was you.

"Julian?" the shadow was asking in a white room with windows.

"Julian?" the shadow was saying. Only now it wasn't a shadow. There was daylight.

"But where's the baby?" my mouth was asking.

"The baby's right here," the shadow said. "Inside me." But it wasn't your shadow anymore.

"Who is the baby? And what happened to it?"

Now the shadow said, "I don't know what you mean."

I had thought that you were the shadow. I did. Now I thought it was the girl with braids from the back yard. But then my eyes blinked more (concentrating harder) and looked again, and the shadow became S. She was sitting on a chair beside me, stroking my forehead, smiling at me.

My eyes were finally open, but my brain was watching an underwater dream.

"Are you awake?" she asked.

I nodded but I couldn't feel my head move.

"I found you two nights ago. What were you doing? You could've killed yourself. Do you always collapse in hallways?"

My mouth was dry, but I moved it.

"Waiting for someone."

"Your M?"

I nodded.

"It's okay. I know you can't talk," she said. "I know you're not too good at it anyway and you're pretty sick right now."

"Why are you here?" I asked.

"I told you," she said. "Weren't you listening? Anyway, I always wanted to see what Wheeling looked like. So here I am."

"How did . . ." but the rest of the question wouldn't come.

"When I heard you ran away, I decided that as long as I was leaving home too, I'd come and find you and maybe we could have a good long talk. I figured that you'd be in Wheeling, working at a McDonald's. I was just about right. They told me you disappeared from there, but at least they gave me your address. That's when I showed up that night. You know, I thought you were dead, lying there like that. I thought I was too late."

She was squeezing my hand and wiping away tears and smiling all at the same time.

"You'll probably think I'm crazy, but I've been thinking — it's a long bus ride to Wheeling, you know — what if we helped each other? What if we tried? Nobody else is going to help us. You'll think I'm crazy but we could get jobs and make some money and then in about seven months we can go our own ways because you probably wouldn't want a baby around. But you're the weirdest, nicest person I've ever met and the biggest puzzle I've ever tried to solve and

I think we make sense — at least for a while."

My ears were running to keep up with her words.

"What do you think? They say you can leave tomorrow if you start walking."

"I don't know," I said.

"What don't you know?"

"I don't know if I'm finished with everything."

"Like what? Looking for your M?"

"Yes," I said.

"Is she here?"

My brain knew what to say, but it was my H that said, "Not really." Then I said, "My M is D." The words echoed in my H.

"I know," she said. "You don't have to say anymore. I found your NBs and I read them. I know about you now. I mean, I think I do. I know about your M."

"Where are they?" I asked.

"Right here," she said. She pulled them from her purse and handed them to me.

"I bought you another NB. I figured you'd want to write about what happened after you left Arizona. It doesn't have a lot of pages, but it has a shiny gold cover. I thought it should be special."

She held up the NB to show me, and suddenly I was

thinking of everything I wanted (and didn't want) to write. I never thought I'd write again after I left home.

"So many strange things happened," I said.

"Don't tell me," she said. "Just write it. When you feel like it. This can be NB #3."

She handed me the gold NB then. The cover was so shiny that I could see my face. I looked thin (thinner than usual) and tired, but very free.

"I think you need some albondigas," she said.

And so we made plans. S had already paid another week's rent on the apartment, so I ate and walked and drank in order to recover. S bought me some Kmart and thrift shop clothes and shoes. Then one day I got dressed and walked (unseen) out of the white UFO room.

We went straight to Apartment 7. It was empty, except for the kitchen where S was standing.

She picked up the sunflower pitcher.

"This is nice," she said. "Even with the chip."

"My M had one like that," I said.

"Now you have one like that," she said. She opened the refrigerator and said, "And I need to buy some food. I don't know about you, but I'm starving."

"Yes," I said.

Then she started laughing. Loud, like she had heard a funny joke.

"What?" I asked.

"I keep hearing my M's voice," she said. "I can just see her finding out about the two of us and she's saying, 'Well, that's like the blind leading the blind.' "

I didn't laugh.

"You'd have to know my M," she said. "And I hope that never happens."

"I'm ready to write now," I said.

Then I picked up this NB, sat myself down, and began to write. Everything.

And now I am almost done.

I'm running out of pages to write on. I wonder how this NB will end. There's no one to steal it, no tragic D. I could make one up, I suppose. I could say that I never left home, that I was locked in my room until I killed my F and stepnother, that I am writing this from jail. That would be very dramatic. I could say that the West Virginia police came looking for S and me, broke us apart, sent us packing back to Arizona and our families where we lived in misery for two more years until S (in a depressed condition) killed herself when she thought she would never see me again. That would be very melodramatic. Or I could say that you are alive and well and have been spotted (like Elvis) living in a small town in Kansas and driving a Cadillac. That would be news.

I don't know what will happen.

And that is the truest (and scariest) sentence I can write. We have been here for almost a week (five days now, to be exact). Yesterday (after S came home from McDonald's), we walked to Greenwood. We were standing on you at 4:23 WP (around sunset).

"Jennifer Sayre Drew," S said.

"Yes," I said.

Then she reached over and took my hand and squeezed it. She didn't say anything else. She just stood there with me, watching and waiting. When I was ready to go, she left without saying another word. She must have had many questions, but she never asked them. Which is good, because some questions take forever to answer. And I have so many about you.

Afterward, we took National Road back to Apartment 7. My brain was thinking that it doesn't know many roads. The road back to Arizona, the road to

Grandma's Attic or Greenwood or Steenrod. Maybe S and I will learn some new roads (together?).

But whatever road I take, I will always expect to find you at the end of it. Your arms are always waiting behind each unopened door, your face behind every shadowy window.

And the day that I find you, you will kiss and hug me and tell me that you missed me so much and that you never intended to leave without saying goodbye or causing me such pain. You will say, Come home with me. And you will take me back to our old house (no more Raymonds) and we will live together and take care of each other forever.

But how long is forever?
And how long do I have to wait?

When I close my eyes and fall asleep now, I am not in the room of the thousand dreams or darkest nights anymore. I am in the room of newspaper beds and chipped sunflower pitchers and Portrait of Jennie — and S. No one knows what will happen in this room or on the roads we find.

Not even us.

All I know is one thing:
This is not the end